BLUEBIRD

FLOWN

Natalie Buske Thomas

DEDICATION

To Brent, Cassandra, Nicholas and Savannah

Special Thanks to Celebrity Guest Characters
Bob Krejcarek
Eric Dittelman

Congratulations Serena Wilcox Pet Contest Winners
1st place winner Finn (entered by Christine)
2nd place winner Toby (entered by the Sharot family)
3rd place winner Roxy (entered by Marie)

I especially want to thank everyone who is a part of "Team Nat". You make a difference in my life.

AUTHOR'S WORKS

Serena Wilcox Dystopian Thriller Trilogy:
Angels Mark, *Covert Coffee*, *Bluebird Flown*

The Serena Wilcox Mysteries: Books 1, 2 & 3
prequels, novellas: *Gene Play, Virtual Memories,
Camp Conviction* (early works)

Other Works: Oil paintings on exhibit (most notably
Savannah Reading in the Butterfly Garden); Non-
fiction *Fred Born Gifted, The Miracle Dulcimer*;
Juvenile Fiction *The Magic Camera*; Comic
Dramatic Mom; Interactive Reading Game *Serena
Wilcox Choose Your Own Mystery Game*

Natalie is also a vocalist, public speaker and
entertainer.

www.nataliebuskethomas.com

RESEARCH CREDITS

The Righteous Mind: Why Good People are Divided by Politics and Religion by Jonathon Haidt
Democracy in America Vol. 1 by Aexis de Tocqueville

PROLOGUE

"We better get moving," said Estep. He signaled to his team via an old school radio cuff. "Bluebird is on the move."

"Bluebird?" asked Serena.

"You," said Estep. "You're my new assignment. Operation Bluebird."

Beav's laugh began as a snorting sound and developed into an all-out guffaw.

"Laugh it up. My bonus for protecting Ms. Bluebird is paying for new tires on my car," said Estep.

The three of them set out together, joined by Agent Bonifield and Agent Champlin. They drove in two separate sedans and maintained a mostly silent journey for the entire two hour trip from Chicago to a rural stretch of road in Indiana. Upon arrival they all got out to stretch their legs and breathe the Hoosier air. Row after row of corn went on as far as the eye could see, and since the farmland was entirely flat, with barely any discernible slope, the Supporters could easily be anywhere. They could be watching them right now from only a few feet away, completely camouflaged. The three agents, and one former agent, were well aware of this possibility. While each of them had served in war zones, and all had been in situations of high pressure, it was the corn that struck their hearts with terror.

Serena's digi watch lit up. "Estep, who knows this number?"

"No one." He grabbed her arm. The watch, too big for her wrist, slid down her hand and fell onto the ground. "Don't pick it up!"

"Shouldn't I answer it? What if it's them?"

Serena didn't know how to answer the call on the digi watch so after a few seconds of fumbling with it Beav grabbed the watch. He knew exactly what to do because, like most contemporary government projects, he had been involved in the design of it.

"Hello?" she said.

"We wanted you to come alone, and without communication."

"Sorry, I couldn't do that."

"We expected as much."

"Then why did you even ask it of me?"

"It cut back on how much we have to deal with. All you have is the watch, correct?"

"Yes. How did you know about it?"

"One of us was in prison. But don't worry, we aren't violent."

"How did you get the number?"

"They are all coded in a series. We tried several until one went through."

Serena racked her brain to think of more ways to stall, more hints about who they were, anything! "Where are you?" She looked around her, as if expecting them to pop out in front of her from behind the corn stalks.

"Leave the watch behind, no tracking devices. Enter the corn row immediately in front of you. Keep moving down the row until you see

3

an arrow on the ground. Follow the arrow. No agents. If anyone is with you, we will leave without meeting with you."

"Maybe we should call off the meeting. If you were honestly trying to help, you would have no issue with federal agents I can personally vouch for."

"No agents – those are our terms."

"I can't agree to that."

The line was disconnected.

At that moment they heard the sound of tires crunching over gravel. Everyone watched as a government issue sedan slowed and then stopped a few yards from where they were gathered. The back door opened and a man exited the vehicle, a man they all recognized instantly as Carson Landon. They all stood stock still with their jaws dropping as they watched him walk toward them. He was unhurried, taking care to protect his $700 loafers.

"Is that who I think it is?" Serena asked rhetorically.

Carson held his hand out to her. "Carson Landon."

Serena stumbled over what to say. "How?

How did you find us and what are you doing here?" She looked around her at the faces of everyone on the team—all looked completely baffled by Governor Landon's sudden appearance. She reached out to accept his handshake, but found something already in his hand.

"That should explain what I'm doing here. The 'how I found you' part is easy: we've had a tracer on your car." Carson pointed to the car that had been assigned to Agent Estep. "I have to say, you ruined my undercover work. The agents who recruited me are not happy. If one government hand would talk to the other every now and then we'd avoid these things."

Serena examined the object in her hand: a single sheet of paper folded several times over. She unfolded it and saw Paul's familiar handwriting. "One of the missing pages from Paul's journal!"

"Yes, this is the page that they didn't want you to see. Paul sent me a message telling me where to find his journal. He suggested that I keep this page in case I needed it." Carson folded his arms across his chest and waited for

Serena to read the journal entry.

She addressed the entire team. "You'll need to verify this of course, but I can tell that the page I'm holding is from Paul's journal. He writes, 'The governor is working undercover. This will probably cost him politically. I wouldn't be surprised if I have him as a cellmate one day, but he's the only one that could pull this off I suspect. Nice to know there are good guys left in politics after all, although Carson Landon should have been VP. They'll find out that Morgan Canon was a big mistake. By then, it could be too late. I'm doing my part to write everything down. I will ask to speak with Serena Wilcox when the time is right. Until then, I'll continue reporting what I see, and I'll let the Supporters know about the governor's involvement.' He signed it and dated it. This was from over a month ago."

Carson cut an attractive figure against the backdrop of the orange sunset sitting on the rural horizon, a view completely unobscured by buildings or even trees. As far as the eye could see there was nothing but farmland, corn, and blue sky that was beginning to darken. Carson stood tall in his crisp navy suit and slim coordinating silk tie. His hair blew in the gusts of wind that sporadically came and went, looking like a male model posing for a calendar cover. Carson, the assembled team, and the government sedans were all in disharmony with the farm scene.

Beav, never intimidated by powerful people, asserted himself. "What is your connection to the Supporters?"

Carson frowned. "I'm not affiliated with the Supporters, but I know who they are, and that's why I'm here. You need to stay away from them."

"Tell us about them," said Serena.

"They are vigilantes who don't believe that government can police itself. While we want the same things, we disagree about how to make those things happen. I work within the system…" Carson let his sentence dangle while he shrugged.

"And they don't. I see. You came all this way to warn us about them?" Serena fixated on the sinking sun behind him. Soon they would be standing amongst the corn in complete darkness, not a house around for miles.

Carson launched into a speech. "Morgan Canon is obviously out of the picture—I do know what happened, by the way, and I even know what almost happened. Beav, I know who you are, and what you did. Thank you for your service. I know you can't be reinstated, but I'd like to thank you on behalf of all Americans, and if there's anything I can do for you, let me know. As far as I'm concerned my role is done, and so is yours. President Kinji is well satisfied with what you did, and she specifically requested that none of you run this thing so far into the ground that you dig up new problems. You got lucky. None of you were hurt. But it could have gone either way."

Estep didn't know if he should refute the claim or let it slip away unchallenged. He settled for a response that was somewhere in the middle. "Are you saying that you were working for President Kinji all along?"

Carson nodded slowly, a gesture that irked Estep. Carson did his best to smooth the team's ruffled feathers. "Don't take it personally guys. President Kinji needed you and you were there for her. I was on a parallel team, the official one. You see, there needs to be some, shall we say 'discretion', in how details are recorded, reported and investigated. For example, as you probably already guessed, it is better for the president that former agents are ghosts. That was, after all, what you signed up for. Covert Coffee needs to go dark. And, actually, it's time for Covert Coffee to end---when the Supporters came up on my radar I came here to close the operation in person, before you peel a new layer of the onion."

Serena extended her hand to Carson; this time his hand was free of paper and he shook it. "Thank you for telling us this in person."

"Of course. Again, thank you on behalf of all Americans. While they may never learn what it is that you did to protect President Kinji and our nation, those of us who know what you did will certainly forever appreciate your service." Carson flashed them the smile of a man who might one day run for president and spun on his heels the best he could on dry husks of corn. He strode to where his driver had been waiting, his shoes somehow managing to make a clicking sound, unless Serena imagined that sound.

As soon as the governor's car was out of sight and the team was preparing to head out themselves, the Supporters called. The voice on the line said, "Serena, take me off speaker. And hold the watch to your ear."

Serena looked at Estep and Beav. Neither objected. At this point, what would it hurt to hear him out the rest of the way? Besides, the longer they kept the line open the easier it would be for agents, the officially active ones, to catch them. Agent Bonifield and Agent Champlin indicated that they were paying attention.

Serena pressed the watch to her ear. "You're off speaker."

"Mommy!" An unmistakably familiar voice rang out, there were a few seconds of dead air, and then the call was disconnected.

A chill went through Serena's body and her fingers struggled to hold the watch. Her face froze. Her mind was a carnival of lights and sounds, but she willed herself into control. *First, steady yourself. You can't let the team know that you heard the voice of your baby girl.*

Serena gave the watch to Beav. Estep noted

her expression and said, "What did he say to you?"

"I'm supposed to go in there, in the corn, to meet with them. I need to go alone."

Estep shook his head. "They said more than that to shake you up this much."

"The digi watch gave me a jolt when I had it next to my ear. Static electricity or something, still feeling it," said Serena.

Beav's eyebrows shot up in an unspoken question. Serena answered with a scowl. This exchange went unnoticed by the others who were already peering through the corn for any sign of the Supporters, but Beav understood her perfectly: *don't say anything*.

"I'm going in there now. Don't follow me; they won't talk to me if you do."

"I don't feel good about this," said Estep. "The governor made it clear that Covert Coffee is over, and the order to desist came down from President Kinji."

Beav jumped in, "The official team, as the governor called it, still wants the Supporters. She can at least get the ball rolling for them while we're here. If she doesn't come out in fifteen minutes we'll go after her."

"Five. Daylight's all but gone," said Estep.

"Split the difference—ten. Give me ten minutes before you go in." Serena didn't wait for an answer but disappeared into the corn.

Estep timed Serena's absence to precisely five minutes. "That's it, we're going in."

Beav grasped Estep by the arm and pulled him away from the team. "Unless you have any objections I'd like to lead."

"Beav, what's going on? Covert Coffee is over, you know that. You can't be reinstated. Let's get Serena and move on." Estep shined a light into the blackness of the corn, illuminating nothing but corn and mud.

"Covert Coffee has become Operation Bluebird Flown." Beav added his light to Estep's, doubling the glare on the cornfield.

"No need for a mission. I'll get her home in time to watch the late show if you stop holding me back."

"No, she's long gone," said Beav.

"What are you talking about?" Estep stopped dead in his tracks.

"He was lying. Check with President Ann. Carson Landon was in the crack in the SM Channel, I don't have to tell you that." Beav looked back at the row of government vehicles; all was quiet.

"He said he was working undercover." Estep said slowly, the words forming in his mouth as his brain ferreted out the truth. "But no one checked his story." Estep bolted into the corn.

Beav, a runner, was smaller and lighter than Estep. He navigated the corn rows easily. He snagged the back of Estep's shirt and yanked him to a stop. "Wait! Let me lead this. I can't be reinstated, my career is over anyway. You can walk away from this right now."

Estep turned to face Beav. "Why did you let her go in there? What else aren't you saying?"

"They have her family."

1

President Ann Kinji had requested a private meeting with Agent Estep. Yet when he arrived in her office, he was taken aback by how many people were crammed in what was usually a spacious room. He tried to do a quick head count and gave up. Thirty? Forty? Obviously this meeting was anything but private.

"Sit or stand, your choice." Ann stared intently at the one empty chair at the table. Estep sat.

"We're ready for you, Madam President,"

said someone with a grating voice and oddly rectangular-shaped head. On his command the wall of screens behind President Ann Kinji illuminated the darkened room.

Estep recognized the information on the display as "the crack in the Social Media Channel". The crack was a virtual hang-out for people who didn't want their conversations tracked. The highest levels of government were well aware of the crack, but were leaving it alone for now to spy on it. Hackers would likely detect Big Brother's presence within the week, and promptly clear out, but until then gathering intelligence was as easy as staring at a screen; watching a feature presentation in which every character incriminates himself. Estep half expected popcorn to be served.

President Ann stepped in front of the wall of screens, a movement that created a flurry of chain reaction as every person in the room leaned forward at rapt attention. She subconsciously tossed her famous Kinji-cut locks – a simple bob made glamorous by a sheen that was born out of a combination of genetics and healthy living.

Ann addressed everyone in the room with an intensity that dressed each person down individually and intimately. "I called you here today to get all of this out in the open. Some of you were involved with Operation Covert Coffee. In a nutshell, Covert Coffee exposed a conspiracy to assassinate the President, which would be me."

An audible collective gasp went up.

Ann waved her hand, a flick of the wrist that was another of her trademark gestures. "Oh don't insult my intelligence by pretending that you didn't know; move on from that quickly, ladies and gentlemen. I'll get right down to it: As President of the newly Re-united States of America, I am nothing more than a figurehead. Perhaps that's been true throughout all of American history, but clearly we have a problem."

Ann paused and peered into the full room at her captive audience. Nothing was heard except for the sounds coming from a heavy breather who was whistling through clogged sinuses with every breath. Heads turned toward the offending breather. Ann redirected their attention to the front of the room.

"It's time for a Show and Tell demonstration. Let me introduce all of the main players in our little game we call government. First, we have the presiding officer of the chamber, the Speaker of the House, who is third in the line of succession to the Presidency. Give us a wave, Joe."

Speaker of the House Joseph Smythe stood, waved, and grinned. He was received by a few snickers and a lone round of applause. He sat back down.

"Shall we begin with a history lesson? The Constitution doesn't require that the Speaker be an elected Member of Congress. Nonetheless, no non-member has ever been elected to the office until this administration. Naturally the norm is that members of the House vote for their own party's candidate, but apparently this time around there was opposition to electing the party's favorite – Joseph Smythe is not a Member. Several within the majority party refused to jump on board and therefore were penalized: they were stripped of seniority and all committee posts.

Make note of these issues I've highlighted for you. Mr. Speaker Joseph Smythe was elected as a non-member, his appointment was not well received by many members of his own party, and, most importantly, after the Vice President, Mr. Speaker is next in line for the office of the presidency.

Please stand, Mr. Speaker of the House, Joseph Smythe. In fact, do us a favor and step forward. Stand next to me. You'll be forming a line right here, boys." Ann's gesture looked like she was ground guiding a fork truck.

Smythe sauntered over to the exact spot Ann pointed out to him. If he resented being brought to the head of the class like a naughty schoolboy, it didn't show on his face or in his demeanor.

Smythe was a man of average height, but had the appearance of looking much taller due to his lanky frame. His boyish face was out of sync with the medium-brown hair that was graying at the temples. He wore a well-tailored suit that had been purchased off-the-rack, tweaked by a skilled tailor and carefully selected to bring out the blue in his eyes. His eyes dropped slightly at the corners, but turned up significantly when smiling. The creases on his face indicated that more smiles than frowns had aged him.

Ann stood much shorter next to Smythe, which gave Smythe a fatherly look. She faced the crowded room that was growing uncomfortably warmer with each passing minute.

"Continuing on, in both pre-'Big War' United States and now, the role of the speakership of the House is this: He actively works to set a party's legislative agenda; the office is endowed with considerable political power. Let me cite an example of a time in American history when the Speaker of the House was a controversial figure. Tip O'Neill comes to mind. O'Neill opposed the policies of President Ronald Reagan; challenging Reagan on defense expenditures, among other things. He was notorious for kicking up a fuss.

Smythe, like Tip O'Neill from days gone by, has actively opposed many of my policies. It is important to note that Joseph Smythe has an impressive amount of influence in the House and Senate, as well as the respect of the media. His rhetoric is more often quoted than any other political figure, barring yours truly."

Smythe stood and pantomimed tipping a hat at the crowd. Polite laughter briefly surfaced but was stopped cold when Ann pierced the mirth with one reproachful gaze.

"Let's move along from Mr. Speaker. I call Vice President Lehman to the front. I don't need to tell you that Lehman is next in line to the presidency. However, he is a new appointment, and my personal choice – we can dismiss Lehman as a threat for these and other reasons. I want him up here for a different reason. He is a stand-in for the VP that many of you seated right here in this very room wanted in this position instead of Lehman.

As you can see, Lehman is holding a sign with a familiar face on it. Surely you recognize that face?"

Lehman had made his way through the packed room and was now standing on the other side of Smythe. He held a poster print of Governor Carson Landon at chest-level. Carson's face flashed a campaign trail smile. In contrast to the Carson sign he displayed,

Lehman kept his own face expressionless. He selected a focal point on the back wall and stared at it while Ann resumed her presentation.

"To be clear: forget Lehman. Focus on Carson, that's who is represented here in this line-up. We know that Carson was talking to someone from the Global Oil Initiative in the crack in the Social Media Channel. I have it on the screen right now. Let's read it together, shall we?"

Ann nodded to her IT right-hand man who promptly loaded the file that Ann had ordered shortly before the meeting. The file had been quickly converted from text-only to text-to-speech. It now scrolled across the wall of screens while audio narrated the dialog between Carson and an unknown person:

45671: "It's going down at the Global Oil Initiative."

23987: "I want assurances."

45671: "I can't do that. I've been told she'll name me as the VP selection at GOB. I can't verify it."

23987: "We need you in."

45671: "I know that."

23987: "We're down to a year. She won't be out of office before the agreement, she needs to be taken out."

45671: "I know, you've made yourself clear. I told you, I'm working on it."

23987: "The last guy we tapped got cold feet, and now his toes are tagged."

45671: "Don't threaten me."

23987: "I'm not. I'm telling you what will happen if you don't hold up your end of our arrangement."

45671: "I have no intention of backing out. I stand to benefit just as much as you do."

23987: "Good to know."

45671: "She contacted me right away. I don't think Morgan's body was even cold yet. No one will be surprised, she talked to the media about me a couple of weeks ago. All looks good."

23987: "Then what's the problem?"

45671: "I'm saying I can't guarantee it. She could change her mind last minute. I've done my part."

23987: "There's no one else she's even mentioned as a VP choice, no one but you."

45671: "Even so, I'm saying I can't guarantee it. I can only say that it looks like a done deal. She's announcing at the press conference at GOB."

23987: "That would be immediately following the initiative then."

45671: "I assume."

23987: "All interested parties will be at GOB."

45671: "I know that."

23987: "They expect to see you."

45671: "I'll be there."

23987: "In person meets are discouraged obviously, but they'll be watching you."

45671: "What are you telling me?"

23987: "Look sharp."

45671: "You contacted me. I told you all I know. What are you saying?"

23987: "Some don't trust you. Watch your back."

45671: "I told you that I'm on board. I've done all that you have asked. Are you telling me that they might kill me anyway?"

23987: "That's what I'm telling you."

45671: "I don't know what more I can do to

gain their trust."

23987: "Turn up, be ready to give assurances."

45671: "I said I'd be there."

"All of this was discovered in Operation Covert Coffee. The GOB initiative went off without a hitch, and Carson Landon was not present at the event. However, Carson is still out there, and I want to know what he's up to. His week-long retreat away from the Governor's mansion was scheduled months in advance, supplying him with a reason for his absence. But he's not there. No one has arrived at the vacation home on his itinerary.

Our last contact with him was when he turned up during the investigation I referred to earlier, Operation Covert Coffee. Classified at a security level that most of you here don't have-- and never will have-- clearance for, you shouldn't know anything about this, but I have a strong feeling that you do."

The sound of rustling feet and throat clearing confirmed her suspicions. She paused, narrowed her eyes in accusation, then resumed speaking.

"How did Carson know where to find my

team? How did he get involved? And where is he now? I need answers."

Ann studied her fidgeting audience before resuming. "I notice a number of raised eyebrows on your faces – which has also been duly noted by my expert profilers, courtesy of the FBI." Ann indicated two people in suits, one male and one female, each positioned to view everyone in the room.

"Ah, surprised again, I see. All of you have been under observation from the moment you stepped into the room. Your reaction to my inquisition into the whereabouts of Governor Carson Landon might reflect your innocence, or it might not.

Yes, Carson was initially my own preference for VP, and even someone I thought of as a friend. I certainly can't blame anyone else for this predicament.

For those of you wondering about my true feelings about Carson's predecessor, Morgan Canon, what you heard from the media was dead on. Morgan was never my pick; I was vocal about that. I was right not to trust Morgan but wrong about placing my trust in Carson. I shouldn't have believed either of them.

I've always viewed myself as a person who possesses a gift for discernment, but I was way off the mark with Carson Landon. If not for the efforts of all the agents and investigators involved in Operation Covert Coffee, I would have played into your hand. I would have tapped Carson to replace Morgan, which is exactly what you expected me to do.

It turns out that both candidates were in the pockets of the mysterious powers that are operating independently of this office, so if Morgan failed them, they had Carson at the ready. It seems they had a backup to the backup and I fell for it - *both* vice presidential candidates had been purchased by unknown power players. Of course I want to know the name of every person involved.

The most logical place to start is with Carson Landon. Find him and learn the identity of the person he was talking to. Who is 23987?"

There was momentary confusion when several law enforcement heads questioned whether or not they should be popping out of their seats to assemble teams at this exact second, or if the president was not finished with them yet. The restlessness of the crowd created a comical stir.

Ann waited for the noise to settle before she began again. "I'm not finished yet. We need to add a couple more to the line-up.

Before moving on, let's review what any intern should already know: The Vice President of the United States serves as President of the Senate, casting the decisive vote in the event of a tie in the Senate. Wow, how convenient it would be to hand-pick the VP you want casting those precious decisive votes! No wonder our friends wanted to make sure they had a puppet in place.

I'll also remind you that the Senate has the sole power to confirm Presidential appointments that require consent and to ratify treaties, with a couple of exceptions, but you get the idea. The point is, the power the Senate has is considerable, perhaps formidable. And with term lengths six years long, with no term limits, some of our senators have had practically a life-time membership in the Old Boys' Club.

It is with these thoughts in mind that I ask

Senator William Casey and Senator Robert Lorry to come forward. Take your place in line, gentlemen."

Senators Casey and Lorry ambled to the front of the room. They obediently took their place in line, but unlike Smythe, who managed to maintain somewhat of an amused smirk on his face throughout this entire presentation, and Lehman, who remained stoic, both Casey and Lorry held pinched and petulant expressions. Although in all fairness, defensiveness and culpability may not have had anything to do with the reason behind these sour faces; they had looked this way for most of their lives.

"Senators Casey and Lorry, two long-time members representing both sides of the aisle, represent the heart of the Senate. I know that we've reformed and there's not supposed to be definitive party lines anymore, but no one is fooled by these redefinitions. The division in our nation is just as bitter as before the Big War, and new labels aren't going to make that go away. But I digress."

Ann strolled in front of the line of men, all of whom dwarfed her diminutive stature. Yet somehow she remained an intimidating force. She used a sweeping hand gesture to indicate all of them as a whole.

"Take a long look. Is it Colonel Mustard in the kitchen with a knife? Or Professor Plum in the billiard room with a revolver?

I'm calling upon our best people in every agency we currently have, and I'm creating new ones as well – agencies that my hand-picked crew will build from scratch. We have to clean house, and find all those who are working against us, all those with their own agenda, all those working outside of the system, and all those who are traitors to our country! I don't care how big the sweep is, I want every bad apple tossed out.

Agents: cancel all vacation plans and make your apologies now to your family members – you will be living here, and in the field, until our mission is accomplished. Consider this the game of Clue from hell. No one will be let out of the game until we reveal all the cards.

As we begin round one, study the gentlemen in this line-up and then cast an even longer look around this room. These are your suspects.

Finally, hold up a mirror. One of you, more than one of you actually, wants me dead."

2

Beav was in the field and had gone dark – literally. He was mucking about in a corn field in the middle of the night; the moonlight bouncing off of his olive skin, his hairline damp with sweat, his nostrils clogged by gnats and his pulse racing. Serena Wilcox was long gone and Operation Bluebird Flown was well underway. Taking Carson's unintentional advice, Beav and Estep were working together, except that only Agent Estep's role would ever see the light of day. If all went well Beav would remain a ghost.

While Estep, on the official side of this operation, was digesting his thoughts about President Ann Kinji's show-and-tell presentation, Beav was unofficially searching for clues about Serena's disappearance. Using nothing more than a plastic flashlight, which was broken and held together by duct tape, he thought his mission was fruitless until his weak beam of light hit upon something. He recognized the object as Paul's journal page, the page that Serena was reading before she took off into the cornfield to meet the Supporters.

Beav picked up the page, which was now soggy from sitting on the moist ground. He examined the paper the best he could under the circumstances. The first thing he noticed was a black smudge on the back of the paper. He placed his dim flashlight close to the page.

It was a scan-read code, he was sure of it! He pulled his phone out of his pocket. Reading a backlit screen was much easier than reading a page by flashlight. He scanned the page, concerned that the quality of the ink and the dampness of the paper would interfere with reading the code. His fears were unfounded; the code scanned flawlessly.

Beav remained where he stood in the corn field, now oblivious to the unnerving aspects of being alone in the pitch black of rural Indiana (moonlight didn't count in his opinion). He heard and felt nothing as he read the short message from Paul Tracy. His thoughts did drift however to the idea that this discovery might be enough to turn his career around. *Could I be reinstated? Is it too much to hope for?*

The note was short but revealing: "If you found the code on my journal page it means that Carson Landon has gotten to you. The Supporters asked me to play along. They'll take care of it. If this is you Serena, sorry I couldn't give you a heads up. You'll find them at this address."

Boom- that's how it's done! Just like that I've found the big break in the case – in my team of one! Beav entered the address into his phone's GPS app. It popped up as only half a mile away from where he was standing in the corn field! He sprinted out of the field, leaping over mud clods and dodging corn stalks. He had only a ragtag support team at his disposal and none of them had arrived yet. Should he continue solo or wait? *Waiting could cost me the mission.*

His rigorous self-punishing extreme fitness routine had equipped him with an easy run to the farmhouse down the gravel road. He felt a whoosh over his head that may have been a bat in flight, but he didn't let that distraction get to him. It was only as he neared his destination that he slowed his steps, his spirit sinking. This house hadn't seen life in a long time.

Nonetheless, he rapped at the peeling door. A shrill bark jolted Beav into taking an involuntary leap backward, his 5'7 frame busting through a splintered stair rail, landing with a hard thud into the foliage below.

"Who's out there?" A man in his fifties held the door open and flicked the porch light on.

Beav shielded his eyes from the sudden glare. "I'm down here. I busted your railing, sorry about that. Gravity is a harsh mistress."

"What are you doing out here in the middle of the night?" He maintained a solid stance that was neither frightened nor angry.

Beav sized him up. He didn't look like a

farmer, his skin was much too pale to have seen much of the sun. No, this was a man who worked indoors. So what was he doing out here if not farming? Beav knew this had to be the Supporters' safe house, or some sort of operations—Paul hadn't steered him wrong. Also, it was a safe bet that that this guy knew about Paul's message. Beav operated on that assumption when he said, "I found your address on Paul Tracy's journal page. Let me in so we can talk."

He nodded and walked back inside, leaving the door open for Beav. Beav followed him into a living room area that was crammed with furniture – clearly Beav's initial impression that the house was abandoned couldn't have been further from the truth. The pet that had sent Beav hurling off the porch with his well-timed bark was a well-groomed toy poodle sitting innocently on a sofa pillow. Littered throughout the room were toys belonging to children and the dog. It was hard for Beav to distinguish the difference between the two.

"I'm Bob. Pull up a seat and start talking." He indicated the high-backed chair nearest to the door for Beav. Bob sank into the sofa, which was an invitation for the poodle to jump into his lap.

Beav sat in the chair offered to him, grateful for a rest. He had been in that corn field for six hours. He'd been near the end of his stamina and patience when he finally found the journal page, a page he now realized that Serena probably left behind for him to find, maybe even upon instruction from the Supporters. This obvious bread crumb didn't make the discovery any less his, a less dedicated field investigator would have missed it. No, he could rightfully claim this one. This single page from Paul's journal broke the case wide open, making his hours in the muddy field worth the fatigue, soiled jeans, chilled extremities, and sore muscles. Sweating while simultaneously freezing was a condition worthy of hazard pay in his opinion, and yet he would have done it all over again for that moment of glory when he found the page.

He couldn't wait to update Estep. Could Operation Bluebird be wrapped up before the end of the week? If so, it would be good news for Serena Wilcox, but bad news for him. He might need to line up a new freelance job sooner than he expected. Beav knew he'd be let go as soon as his services were no longer needed; let go, and never heard from again. He was torn between excitement about how fast this case was wrapping up and despair at the thought of his impending unemployment. *The money was good while it lasted.*

"I'm waiting. A name would be nice." Bob was staring at Beav, and had been for a couple of minutes or more.

Beav shook off his brain fog. "This was the address on the journal page."

"Yes, you said that. Who are you? Who do you work for?"

"People call me The Beav. I'm looking for Serena Wilcox."

"How do I know she wants to be found?"

"She's my friend."

Bob rubbed his chin, a motion that had less to do with deep thinking and more to do with soothing a raw skin patch due to a recent shave. "Give me more."

"I'm not going to hurt her. I think we are on the same side in this."

"That's what I'm trying to figure out but you aren't giving me much to go on." Bob rubbed the poodle's belly after the little dog flopped over, begging for attention.

"Ask me anything you want to know."

Bob told the dog to sit. When the poodle was settled he asked, "Who do you work for?"

"I can't fully answer that," Beav said without any hint of irony in his voice.

"What good is asking you questions if you aren't going to answer? How long are we going to be at this?"

Beav eyed him critically. "What do you do?"

"Not that I need to answer you, given that you aren't forthcoming with information yourself, but I don't see the harm. I'm a radio host."

"Internet radio?"

"No, old school radio broadcasting."

"People still do that?"

Bob mimicked Beav's tone. "Yes, 'people still do that'."

"Where do you operate out of?"

"Here."

"On this property?"

"Here in this house. I have a studio downstairs."

"You have a studio in the basement?"

"Yes."

"What for? Is there a market for this?"

Bob held up his index finger. "It's my turn. Why are you here, who are you working for, and why are you looking for Serena Wilcox? You have to give me something or I'm going to ask you leave."

"Serena was taken by the Supporters. This address is what I found when I was looking for her. That's all I know. I'm assuming you know how to find the Supporters, and Serena."

"I thought it might be something like that. Am I to assume you are working for the government – our home government?"

"As opposed to what? A foreign government?"

"So that's a yes."

"I really can't say." Beav had grown restless with the conversation. He roamed about the room, studying the pictures on the walls and piecing together the people who lived here. He shook his left leg which had fallen asleep and was now tingly.

"All right then, tell me what you know about Carson Landon."

"I know that he's a bad dude."

"You aren't working for Carson?"

"No." Beav saw so much evidence of Bob's life through the framed portraits on the walls that he didn't feel the need to investigate further. Bob wasn't a threat to anyone. From what Beav could see, he was a family man and even a pillar of the community, according to the awards and plaques filling up what little space remained after all of the family pictures. What Bob was doing with the Supporters was the question of the hour. Nothing about him screamed radical.

Unlike Beav, who had dismissed Bob as a person of interest, Bob's radar was on full alert. "Wait a minute, I recognize you. Weren't you involved with the infamous Paul Tracy bombing? Your face was all over the news. Is that your connection to Paul?"

Beav picked at the dried mud on his jeans. He made a note to self to alter his appearance. Who would have thought that he would be recognized? He hadn't really been "all over" the news; to the best of his knowledge his mug had only appeared once, for maybe a millisecond. "Hmm, you've got me. Yes, I'm that guy."

"They let you back in? I'm surprised you aren't in prison alongside Paul." Bob stroked his chin again.

"This should prove I'm on the right side."

"Not necessarily. Carson Landon has a lot of influence. He could get you a get-out-of-jail-free card."

"This has become tedious. Trust your gut. Which side do *you* think I'm on?" Beav didn't know how the tables had been turned on him, but he wouldn't be mentioning this part of his investigation in his report.

"You don't seem the type who would align himself with an entitled politician like Carson, but you don't look like you're active government either." Bob's eyes flitted to Beav's ponytail. "That's not a regulation haircut."

Beav touched the tip of his nose, charade-speak for "on the nose". With his hair pulled back he looked less agent and more gypsy, which suited him much more than the crew cut and suit ever had.

"You're not working for *any*one are you? You've gone rogue?" Bob glanced into the kitchen, wondering how close to the top of the silverware drawer his knives were.

"I'm not rogue. I am unofficial, for the protection of all involved. I'm one of the good guys. My back-up team will be here any minute. That should confirm what I'm saying."

Bob was at Beav's side in a flash, yanking him up on his feet by the arm. "Come with me." He dead-bolted the door, turned off all the lights, scooped up his little dog and led Beav to the stairs tucked into the back of the front entry closet. Hidden behind rows of coats, the stairs were effectively camouflaged.

Bob spoke quickly in a raspy whisper, "Keep quiet and I'll try to help you."

Noise wasn't an issue. The likelihood of being discovered after they were sequestered downstairs was practically nil. Besides, Beav knew his team wouldn't search that hard for him; if they found the house vacant, they'd do a cursory search, then call him, and then leave-regardless of whether he answered his phone or not. Bob had probably already thought of that himself. Beav's mind raced. Why *was* Bob here all alone in the middle of nowhere? Maybe Beav had dismissed him too soon. Where was the family in the pictures? Had Bob done something to them? Beav chided himself: he was sleep deprived. Nonetheless, he slipped his hand into his pocket and felt the reassurance of his favorite weapon – a humane gun; it shot tranquilizer darts that were effective on animals and humans alike.

In the bellows of the house, inside a windowless room with walls that had been modified with sound-proofing material, Beav felt silly. Besides the silence, nothing about Bob's basement studio screamed serial killer. Beav looked the equipment over and gave a low whistle. "You aren't playing around."

"This is my livelihood."

"And you do what? DJ?"

"Yes, and I host a talk show, I flip the switch on syndicated programming, I do everything else you might expect from radio." Bob slid behind his desk and sat down. He put his headset on.

"Why are you doing this from here?" Beav genuinely admired the equipment, and even fleetingly wondered if he might like to have a show of his own. Although much of the technology was now considered obsolete, he saw a few top of the line cutting-edge items in the mix. The cool toys alone made the gig appealing.

"I'm on a frequency no longer used." Bob spoke in a clipped hurried tone.

"Hiding from regulation?" Beav forced himself to focus on the investigation; he stopped eyeballing the toys.

"Now you understand." Bob flicked the on-air button.

"And this is how you talk to the Supporters?" Beav noted that Bob was fully suited up for broadcasting.

"This is how they talk to me, yes."

"Contact them now, tell them I found Paul's code."

"It doesn't work that way. They contact me. They phone in during my show, always from a different phone. They are careful. Don't bother trying to find them. They'll call."

"How long do we have to wait? I can't dodge my team forever. They'll send out the alarm if I don't check in within the hour."

"I thought you were operating on your own."

"No, not on my own. I said I'm operating 'unofficially'."

"What does that mean?"

"I have a team, I have people to report to. It's organized." Beav searched for a way out of the studio. The windows seen from outside the house were blocked by the sound proofing material.

"You're trying to take down Carson Landon?"

"Not me. My objective is to get Serena Wilcox back."

"That's going to be a problem," said an unknown voice that suddenly boomed at them from the surround sound system.

"You represent the Supporters?" Beav asked, to confirm what was obvious. Apparently Bob had been broadcasting their conversation.

"You know who we are. And you also know that we wouldn't hurt Serena." The man's voice wasn't digitally disguised. He sounded unhurried and in control.

"You took her child. She's with you now

45

because you held her child as leverage." Beav's mind raced. He couldn't get a read on this guy.

"I regret that we needed to do that, but we didn't hurt her family. They understood that we needed her to believe that we might. Her little girl is quite an actress."

"You are telling me that Serena and her entire family are OK?" Beav was going off the play book: verify that Serena is still alive.

"Yes." The man's voice didn't reveal anything. He was either telling the truth or he was a sociopath.

"Why won't you put her on the phone?"

"She's occupied."

"With what?"

"Preventing the take-down of the United States." The man's tone held not a hint of sensationalism.

"Another attack?" Beav looked at Bob. Bob was somber and his body language looked like that of a person attending a funeral. What that meant was impossible to guess.

"No. A buy-out."

"A what?" Beav continued to monitor Bob's reaction, but Bob was giving nothing away, if he even knew anything at all.

"Foreign investors." The representative of the Supporters had a smooth speaking voice with excellent diction.

"I still don't understand." Beav admitted.

"I don't have time to explain this to you. Serena has agreed to help."

"Put her on the phone."

"I can't do that."

"Why not?"

"She isn't here."

"Where is she?" Beav didn't expect a direct answer, so what he heard next sent his head spinning:

"She's with Carson Landon."

3

Carson Landon was not happy to see her. Serena smiled at the thought of his displeasure. "Hello, Governor Landon," she said.

"What are you doing here, Ms. Wilcox?"

"I could ask the same of you."

"Is anyone with you?" Landon's eyes darted from left to right and then back again. Given that he didn't move his head, it was a futile attempt to survey the room.

"Oh, you're wondering if I came alone. Don't even think of whatever it is you're thinking of doing. I have people, yes."

Landon folded his arms across his chest in a classic defensive posture that made him look like a B-list actor playing the role of a dirty politician. His dialogue was equally uninspired. "I'm not going to tell you anything. I want you to leave."

Serena laughed. "I'm not going anywhere. You have no power over me." She meant it, he seemed like a cartoon to her now.

"This is private property."

"That's right. And it doesn't belong to you. I have permission to be on these premises. Can you say the same?"

Landon's eyes darted around the room again.

Serena enjoyed watching him squirm. "Don't bother looking for a way out. My people are waiting for you at every exit."

"What is it that you think I can do for you?"

"That's what we're going to do? Pretend that you don't know what I want?" Serena stood with her hands on her hips, her legs locked into a cowboy stance. She held her ground at not quite five two inches tall.

"Tell me what you want and I'll tell you if I

can help you." Carson Landon slipped back into the golden tongue of a practiced diplomat.

Landon's bronzed skin had been fortified by artificial tanning, his hair had been recently styled by a professional who managed to charge five times more money to cut the locks of a governor than the hair of an average citizen, and something about his nose hinted that plastic surgery had created its mannequin-like symmetry and perfection. The total package that was Carson Landon had worked well for him over the years, but somehow his expensive grooming habits didn't do him any favors today. It was as if uncovering his deception had also unveiled the secrets to his empty good looks; revealing him to be the fool that he was.

"Governor, you were identified as one of the voices in the crack in the Social Media Channel, there's no doubt, and I think you know that. The jig is up. You were making plans to become the next Vice President, or should I say lining yourself up to be President? But the assassination attempt on President Kinji was aborted because your puppet masters knew that we were on to them. So now you are here, hiding. You should have played hide and seek more as a child."

"Why isn't anyone arresting me then? Why are *you* here? On that subject, what business do you have in anything at all?"

"I have many talents." Serena started to say more but she thought better of it. Why was she defending herself? Besides, there wasn't much to say. The main reason why President Kinji hired her was because Serena was a person she could trust. In Ann's world, where few people had anything real about them, transparency and honesty were more important than any credential or certification could ever be. But that sounded flimsy even to her own ears.

Serena moved on. "You're in a lot of trouble, and you wouldn't be hiding if you didn't think so yourself. So why don't you stop this nonsense and help yourself?"

"You're offering me a deal? How do I know you're in any position to do that? I'd want it in writing." Landon's expression was pinched, as if he was setting himself up to take the upper hand in a negotiation.

"Oh no, I'm not offering you a deal. That's

never going to happen."

"What are you talking about then?" The mighty governor was indeed a B-list actor; he couldn't conceal his dismay.

"We can protect you from the people you sold out."

"I haven't sold anyone out." Landon's eyes darted. His face reminded Serena of a rabbit's.

"By running here, you all but signed a confession of guilt. It's only a matter of time before you tell us everything, and they know that."

Landon folded his arms across his chest again. He was cycling through his postures and movements like he had choreographed a routine. "They don't know that because it won't happen. I've told them I won't talk."

"And they believed you?"

Carson's face turned gray even under all that fake tan. "Leave me alone."

"I'd love to, but I think you'd prefer to have my help."

"Why would I trust you over them? You'll put me in prison."

Serena smiled until her green eyes sparkled

like a cat who had gotten into the nip. "Definitely. You're going to prison whether you talk to me or not."

"Then put cuffs on me and be done with it." Landon held out his wrists.

"You could go to prison with protection or without it."

"Protection from?"

"From the people you've been working for. Come on, Carson, you can't be that stupid. You do know that they're going to kill you now, right? The sooner they get rid of you the better. They know that you'll talk eventually. Besides, you're no good to them now. You're better off dead." Serena fleetingly wondered if a funeral makeup artist would need to touch him up or if his fake tan would cross over into the afterlife.

"Witness relocation?"

"Never going to happen. You're a traitor."

"I'll take my chances on my own then. You haven't offered me anything." Landon crossed his arms and his eyes darted again in rabbit-like fashion; he had stepped up his routine to include a combo.

"So your plan is what? Carson, I'm not

leaving. My people aren't leaving. There's no escape for you. If you cooperate, you'll go to a special prison where cellmates are heavily protected. If you don't cooperate, your friends will have you killed as soon as you put on your orange jumpsuit, if not before. Do you want to die, or do you want to accept my offer of a VIP prison ticket?"

Carson put his head down in his hands and made a curious sound. Serena realized he was crying. He gasped and shook, sobbing until he was choked up and blowing his nose on a cloth napkin. Serena watched him cry, fascinated by how quickly his arrogance had become pitiful. He croaked out the words, "I want the VIP ticket."

"That can be arranged." Serena grinned. This was her first real interrogation and she had broken her suspect on the first try! Beginner's luck, or did she have the knack? Whichever it was, she took it as a serious win. "All we need from you is a list of names."

"Now?"

"Yes. And while you're at it, why Lehman's house? You knew it would be vacant, but wow, that's brazen. How did you even get in?"

"Celebrity has its privileges. I'm still Governor. I told the house sitter that I was invited here. She didn't bat an eye."

"Did you bat *your* eyes?" Serena knew the effect Carson had on women, but not from personal experience – she couldn't bear his type.

Carson's smile was almost a leer. There was no trace of his tears of ten seconds ago. "Something like that. How did you find me, have you been tracking me?"

"Something like that," she parroted back at him, with equal flippancy. "Give me the list of names."

"Those Supporters were tracking me, weren't they? You talked to them."

"Yes, and yes. The names please? Seriously, Carson, if you don't hurry, you'll be killed before I can help you."

As if on cue, they both heard what sounded like a round of firecrackers. Serena grabbed Carson's hand and pulled him behind the kitchen counter, but it was too late. Carson's eyes were round with the realization of his fate. A second later he was dead.

4

"That's so cliché. He died before giving me the names!" Serena folded her arms across her chest. She dropped her arms the instant she realized that she was adopting the same posture that Carson Landon had repeatedly done just moments before his untimely demise.

Agent Estep raised an eyebrow but didn't ask what her problem was. "You have a track record of informants dying on your watch."

"I'd gotten him to accept the offer."

"Does us no good now."

Serena looked around Lehman's kitchen. The Birmingham area house had a pending offer. She wondered if the blood spatter would complicate the closing. "I know, I know," she said. "I really am sorry."

"Why didn't you call me sooner? I'm not your clean-up crew." Estep maintained his grumpy old man demeanor even though he was almost twenty years her junior. Serena's ditzy personality, irreverent humor, and often insipid methods of investigation drove him to gnash his teeth.

"They asked me not to."

"What, you're working for the Supporters now?" Estep stared at her, his eyes reflecting a hard glint. He had come around to respect her unorthodox methods, and as long as they didn't have to spend too much time together they got along fine. He even enjoyed their repartee—exchanging barbs with Serena reminded him of the energy of his childhood family, his grandmother, his mother and a houseful of sisters; all of them strong and dynamic women. But this time Serena had pushed him too far: she hadn't contacted him since she went missing, not until now when there was a dead governor to take care of.

"*You're* working for the Supporters, since you're official government. They are American citizens, and last I knew, our government works for *us*."

Estep made a big show of expressing that he was dumbfounded. "Have you been sucked into their cult voodoo mind control? I don't work for vigilantes."

"Vigilantes? I wouldn't go that far. They aren't violent or anything like that. I don't even think they are crazy, well, at least not psychotic. There's a higher-than-average OCD vibe coming off those geniuses."

"You're saying that you trust them?" Estep's expression was hard to read but Serena thought she saw something that resembled human warmth. "Why didn't you contact me? We've been looking for you. Beav was in the field most of the night."

"Yes, I trust them. I left Beav a message, didn't he get it?"

"You mean the journal page? Yes, he got it. But you should have called me." Estep's voice trailed off because he was distracted. He was memorizing the crime scene while hashing this out with Serena. While he didn't think there was anything about the scene that would be of any use, he never left anything to chance.

Meanwhile, Serena had ruled out any importance to the crime scene details and had stopped expending energy on thinking about it. She wanted to ask Estep what he planned to do next, but she knew he wouldn't answer her. She had learned from experience that the best way to keep Estep's moods on even keel was to reign in her tendency to babble.

Thirty minutes later Estep finally released the scene at Lehman's house to the FBI investigation team and indicated for Serena to follow him to his vehicle. "Call them and arrange a meeting."

"By 'them' I assume you mean the Supporters?" Serena couldn't imagine who else he could be referring to, but she sought to confirm anything that could come back on her later if she got it wrong.

"You aren't working with them anymore without me there."

"You're worried about me!" Serena exclaimed. So that was the warmth she'd seen in his face!

Estep snorted, grunted, and looked ready to fly into convulsions. "I'll be there to make sure you don't screw this up."

The ride to the nearest fast food restaurant was long. Estep needed coffee, for both of their sakes. He pulled up to the drive-through window, ordered a large black coffee, and drove to the next window without asking if Serena wanted anything.

"Hey, I wanted to order a burger!" Serena yelped.

"You should have said something."

"Can I run in real quick and get one?"

"No."

"What good does it do to say something?"

"You asked too late. I'm already through."

"I can go in right now, won't take long."

Estep locked her door with his panel controls.

"Alrighty then." Serena glared out the window, looking more like a petulant child than a private detective for hire. Glaring was Estep's domain. Her attempts to dish it back out were ridiculous.

Estep paid for his coffee, grabbed the hot foam cup of joe and drank it without hesitation. Whether or not it scorched his throat was impossible to tell. Serena assumed he had built up so much scar tissue from this habit that he no longer felt the burn. Minutes later Estep mellowed out enough to initiate dialog.

"Before Carson kicked off, you had him dead to rights?"

"Definitely, and I recorded the whole thing, but you know that already. Besides, you know he was guilty. Why are you asking me this?"

"I have to be sure."

"There's no doubt." Serena made a crossing motion over her heart.

Estep nodded.

After a few seconds Serena asked, "Aren't you going to tell me what's going on?"

"No."

"What? Come on, I'm on this case too."

Estep pulled the car over gently, smoothly, and only after the flow of traffic allowed for the transition. He slowly set his coffee in the cup holder. He undid his seat belt and twisted his upper body toward Serena. "This is not a case. It is a high-level threat to the President. You are not an agent."

"This is crazy! You know I was a big help with Covert Coffee."

"Random," Estep scoffed.

"Random? What do you mean by that? Come on, you know I was in the middle of that operation. If it wasn't for me…"

"If it wasn't for you, I wouldn't be sitting here right now!"

"What's going on? We were past all of this." Serena searched his face for clues. Again, she found a trace of humanity. "I was right, you are worried about me, aren't you?"

Estep buried his face into the steering wheel, his voice muffled. "You remind me of my grandmother."

"How old do you think I am? I'm barely old enough to have been your mother – maybe not even quite old enough for that. I'd have to do the math."

Estep continued to speak through the steering wheel, his forehead pressed hard against its leather cover. "She was spunky like you, short like you. She was funny and smart, and dead."

"I'm not sure why you felt the need to bring up the height issue, but I'm flattered by the rest. I'm assuming she didn't die of natural causes?"

"No. She got involved in something she shouldn't have messed in. Just like you."

"I'm an incredibly lucky person."

"Luck runs out."

"You can't pull me off this case. I already have authority to be on it."

"I can't be your bodyguard."

"Why not? Isn't that basically what President Ann asked you to do?"

"I can't because you won't follow protocol. You aren't dead right now because of dumb luck."

"Told you, I'm lucky."

Estep withdrew from his position at the wheel and looked her in the eye. "You don't respect chain of command, or me. You are, I repeat, not an agent."

"I do respect you, Estep. I'm sorry I've made you believe otherwise."

Estep made a murmuring sound that may

have been forgiveness. "You'll do it again. There will be another dead body and next time it might be yours."

"I'll work on this with my own team if you aren't willing to help me."

Estep made an utterance that sounded like a strangled sigh, a cat in mid-yawn, or an expletive that Serena had never heard before. Then he snapped his seat belt back into place, turned the key in the ignition and steered the car back onto the freeway.

5

Three hours later, Agent Estep and Serena were at, of all places, the Medieval Times. Just outside Chicago, it offered them easy access from the freeway and a noisy chaotic environment – perfect for meeting with Beav, no one would overhear them here. While they waited for him to arrive they were barely able to hold a conversation over the din. Children ran to and fro, waving flashing wands and fighting with plastic swords. It was a relief when Beav approached them.

"Let's get on with it," said Estep.

They huddled in the midst of the packed lobby, between a souvenir stand and a line of people waiting in the beer line. It was an effective cloak of invisibility.

Beav began. "I spoke with the Supporters, someone named Bob and some other guy who didn't give me his name. They said that there is a financial take-over in the works, orchestrated at high levels of our own government as well as in a joint venture across the globe. We're talking about a buy-out on a scale we've never seen before, of the entire American government and our national business infrastructure. I don't know any details, nor would I likely understand it, but I believe them. Even if they're wrong, we can't ignore that they could be right." Beav had to shout over the sounds of war coming from three hyperactive boys running and jousting in and around their party of three. "And there was never really any threat to Serena's family."

Serena nodded. "Their threat was a carrot to get me to go to them, but Tom and the kids were waiting for me on the other side of the corn – not a scratch on them. All is well."

"Fine, good, I knew that." Estep gave one of the jousting boys his famous glare. The child's eyes flew open wide and he ran away with the other two at his heels.

Unlike Beav and Serena, Agent Estep didn't need to raise his voice; his deep baritone was always inescapably audible. "How did you end up with Governor Landon and why didn't you contact me?"

"What, this again? I left the journal page for Beav. I knew he'd find it and sure enough, he didn't let me down."

Beav mimed taking a stage bow.

Serena continued, "They asked me not to contact anyone until I spoke to Carson Landon myself. They were afraid he'd be tipped off otherwise, and now that he's dead, obviously they were right to be concerned."

Estep wouldn't let it go. "They got to him anyway. Going vigilante did nothing but botch the investigation."

Serena protested, "You don't know that you could have kept him alive any longer than I did. Which makes me question: how did they know I was meeting with Carson? Were they watching me?"

"We'll never know because I couldn't assign you a surveillance team."

Beav finally had enough. "Can we move on from this?"

Estep gave Serena one last dark stare and then complied. "Here's what I've got: President Kinji laid it all on the table. In a nutshell, she accused the whole room of wanting to kill her."

Serena leaned in closer. "Anyone look guilty?"

Estep shook his head. "Profilers didn't see anything, nothing much anyway. Suspects are Mr. Speaker of the House, Joseph Smythe, Governor Carson Landon, who is now dead and worthless to us…"

"I said I was sorry!"

Estep ignored her. "…Senator William Casey and Senator Robert Lorry. But like I said, President Kinji was accusing everybody. No one is above suspicion except for her emergency Vice Presidential appointee Agent Lehman, and yours truly."

"I wish I'd been there," Serena moped.

"President Kinji wants to do something

historic and unprecedented." Estep relished knowing that he had witnessed something Serena would have given her eyeteeth for. He spent a few seconds people watching, letting Serena stew.

"Well, what? What is it?" Serena knew he was dragging out the suspense to get her goat, but she couldn't wait him out.

"She wants to invoke a UN loophole of some kind. She plans to take over the house and senate, temporarily having full authority: the executive branch would have full power to override the congress." Estep gloated- it was fun knowing something Serena didn't.

Beav whistled. "I didn't know she could do that."

Estep said, "It's never been done before. She has to get a UN resolution to pass. If she can manage it she'll be fully in control of the nation."

Serena questioned, more for her own ruminating than for conversational purposes, "What will she do with that power?"

Estep replied, "She'll replace long-time members of congress with newbies, none of them are career politicians. Then she's going to ask them to set term limits."

Beav asked, "Who? The new congress?"

Estep nodded. "Of course the new congress—the old regime would never vote themselves out, that's the point! She wants term limits to protect future generations from this happening all over again. To fix what's already been done, she's flushing congress of anyone who's been there longer than the past two years."

"Wow, I can't imagine they'll go away quietly," Serena worried.

Estep laughed. "If necessary she'll order the Department of Homeland Security to escort them out. All that stockpiling of weapons they put into the DHS back in 2012- bet they didn't expect it to be used against their own decrepit selves!"

"They're going in." Beav moved toward the doors.

Estep shook his head. "No, not yet. She doesn't even have the resolution yet."

Beav pointed at the double doors ahead. "No, I mean here, they're going in. What did you think we were waiting for all this time? That's where the dinner theater is."

"What? We aren't staying." Estep pulled him back.

"I'm starving. We're staying until we eat. I had to buy these tickets, and they weren't cheap. You're lucky they had anything available at the last minute." Beav donned his paper crown and merged with the crowd.

"Lucky." Estep snorted. Hunger weakened his stance. He followed Beav with Serena was close at his heels.

Estep and Serena were prompted by the hostess to put their crowns on. Serena complied, Estep did not. They were led into the arena to their assigned seats, rooting for the yellow knight. Estep sat like a lump until the show began. Then, taking both Serena and Beav by surprise, he got into the whole affair. He was soon bellowing and booing above the rest. He appeared to be having fun, proving that anything is possible. As soon as the food was gone and the show ended, Estep's good humor was turned off like a switch.

"Time to hit the road." Estep glanced around

the arena and was satisfied to find nothing unexpected. They hadn't been followed and they hadn't attracted any attention. Incredibly, the presidents' investigation trio, motley crew that they were, had slipped into The Medieval Times without notice. Slipping back out was just as easy. Of course Estep was the only one of them who looked like (and was) an agent.

"Are we riding together now?" asked Beav.

"What are you going to do with your car?" asked Serena.

"A friend dropped me off," said Beav.

"How did you intend to get back?" asked Serena.

Beav shrugged. "I find a way."

"Doesn't matter. He's coming with us." Estep settled into the driver's seat and waited for Serena and Beav to negotiate who was riding shotgun. Beav won, having longer legs and a better rapport with Estep than Serena had.

It was a relatively short drive to The Cube, but with traffic bumper to bumper the trip took over two hours. By the time they reached the secret entrance to the underground parking garage Estep was intolerant of any sound; radio, talking, even loud breathing. Even before the car came to a complete stop the three of them burst out of it like clowns in a circus act.

They hit the restroom, snack bar and conference room in that order. Armed with coffee and sandwiches, they were ready for a long session of whatever President Kinji had in store for them.

They didn't have long to wait. President Ann, as Americans affectionately called her, was always on time. The three of them stood up when she entered the room. Ann waved her hand dismissively. They sat. Ann cleared her throat and looked at them expectantly.

Serena got the ball rolling. "What we have so far: The Supporters claim that there is a financial takeover brewing; that's what Covert Coffee was about. Governor Carson Landon is dead, but he wasn't a big player anyway."

"It would have been nice to hear what he had to say." Ann scowled.

"I know, I'm sorry." Serena blushed.

Beav took over. "The Supporters gained my respect. I suggest that we assume that what they are saying is the truth until we disprove it."

Ann placed her elbows on the table, folded her hands without lacing her fingers, and rested her chin on her hands. "Who wants me dead and why? Why do I stand in their way?"

The three of them looked at each other, none of them prepared with an answer. After a few awkward seconds lapsed Agent Estep said, "We don't know. That's all we have. Should we talk to the politicians you brought to the front of the room in your briefing?"

Ann closed her eyes. She held that silent position for so long that the three investigators grew anxious. Then she inhaled deeply, exhaled slowly, opened her eyes, and lifted her face from her chin-on-hands pose. "I can't be involved in this."

"Of course not, you're the President," said Beav.

Ann shook her head. "No, I mean that I can't know what you are doing. It's beyond covert. There's literally no one left I can trust. And I was a fool to have thought that there was."

Serena reached across the table and gave Ann's hand a squeeze. "You are no worse off than you were before. You can trust Lehman,

Estep, Beav, myself and child genius Nicholas from the Superman Lab. Tom and my kids are big fans, and your own husband has never given you any reason to doubt his devotion. I could keep going with this; Penny your former driver comes to mind. It's a big circle of trust –bigger than most people have actually, but you know that already. What's really going on?"

Ann locked eyes with Serena. "I'm not leading this country."

Estep stood up. When women started bleeding emotions his instinct was to bolt. President Ann Kinji may be his Commander-in-Chief, but at this moment she was acting like a woman. He knew the signs, having lived in a house full of sisters. "I don't think I'm needed here."

Transparent as he was, Kinji could read Estep like a large-print book. Ann stiffened her spine and gestured for him to sit back down. Then she stood up. "Make no mistake, I'm still leading *you*."

Estep was sufficiently chastised, another familiar scene from growing up with a strong-willed mother, grandmother and sisters. He slumped in his chair, knowing that he may as well be a fly on the wall.

With Estep muzzled, Ann launched into conversation. "To clarify, I've come to realize that the American government has, for longer than I care to think, been manipulated by the powerful few at the top – in congressional seats they've held fast to while presidents have come and gone. The reality is that the office of the presidency has been stripped of power a little at a time, year after year, until it has been diminished to this: I am nothing more than a puppet. I've been like Pinocchio, believing I'm real and then finally waking up to the realization that I've been dancing in a puppet show all along. Well no more! My eyes are wide open, painted wood though they may be."

"Surely it hasn't gotten that bad?" Serena volunteered. "And what about your overthrow of Congress? That had to have helped."

"Yes, it has. Nonetheless, cleaning house is going to be challenging to say the least." Ann stared out her bullet-proof office window, seeing nothing but sky due to being on one of the highest floors of the Cube.

Serena pressed forward. "Question for you: how does the new Congress help us in our efforts?"

Ann raised her eyebrows. "Help us? You mean investigation-wise?"

Serena nodded.

"It doesn't. Congress is to operate as normal. The old guard has been sequestered and the official independent investigation team is questioning them as we speak. Their investigation as well as yours will not further distract the nation from running as usual. Corruption from within has slowed me down throughout my entire presidency. I won't allow it to bog down the remainder of my term, and I won't leave this mess as a legacy for future administrations." Ann had worked herself up into a frenzy and was now pacing back and forth, moving so swiftly that it looked like Serena and Estep were watching a tennis match.

Serena frowned, fearing a tongue lashing. "I understand what you are saying. I'm doing my best to grasp what you want us to do. If we aren't needed to interrogate former members of Congress, or any of the prime suspects, what is it that we should be doing?"

Ann stopped short. "I expect you to figure that out. You three will have the lab at your disposal, a team, and anyone or anything you need. You can have a jet. Just say the word. It's a massive clean-up, and while I have everyone on it, our hands are tied by the law, and soon the media frenzy will slow us down significantly."

"I understand. We'll figure it out." Serena dared to make a promise that she had no idea how to keep.

"We'll start with your line-up then?" Estep asked. He recognized that the conversation had finally come back around to the investigation.

Ann shook her head with enough vigor that her bob shook.

"No?" Estep was baffled. There appeared to be no clear agenda and dragging one out of the president was seemingly impossible.

Beav took a stab at it. "You don't want us going over the same territory as the official investigation team."

Ann gave Beav the thumbs-up sign. "Exactly. My own team can handle the obvious, and following protocol will do. Beyond the obvious? Frankly, if I wanted by-the-book I wouldn't ask for you three: Loose Cannon, Loose Screw and, well, Serena." Ann paused. "Give me crazy. That's what we need."

"I can do crazy," said Serena.

Ann evaluated Serena Wilcox Bridges, former private detective, mother of three, and a person who had become a close friend, as close as anyone could get to Ann Kinji, a woman with an intimidating persona and emotional walls of steel. Serena's green eyes stared back at her, eyes incapable of anything but honesty; silly, raw, human honesty. Yes, Ann was confident she had made the right move.

The President of the United States left the table without another word or a look back. Because the corridor's motion sensors had been turned off for their meeting, Ann rapped on the door for her secret service detail to let her out, leaving the doors wide open behind her. The three remained seated, glancing at each other with raised eyebrows and shrugs.

"I'll take that as our cue to leave," Beav whispered.

Estep and Serena followed him out the door,

down the corridor, and to another secret exit, one that Agent Estep never knew existed, but Serena and Beav had used many times in the past. It was the *secret* secret exit, the one for outsiders to the Cube, for people whose existence would be denied if necessary; for people whose existence would be terminated if necessary.

It was then that Estep understood what President Kinji had done. His career as he knew it was over. He had been cast out – he was dark! His heart sank as he realized that his only hope of ever acting as an official government agent again lay with Serena Wilcox.

6

Serena was back in the Superman computer lab, which had been previously compromised but had been relocated to a new top secret location. It was much closer to The Cube, just three hours' drive, near President Kinji's hometown of Warsaw, Indiana. The lab was in an underground location in the middle of nowhere. The nearest store was in Oswego, a tiny town with few shopping possibilities. Thankfully the lab was fully stocked with anything they could possibly need.

In newly re-united America, post Big War, everything that was D.C. based was now in Chicago. The new Wall Street was in Minneapolis. Because America's headquarters had relocated from the East coast to the Midwest, states beyond Illinois and Minnesota were becoming more important. For example, Indiana, with its state line so near Chicago, was now part of an even bigger sprawl – commuters were buying properties way beyond Gary, Indiana, often commuting three or more hours to work each way. Many employers offered sleeping rooms – commuters living at the workplace, coming home only on weekends or even less frequently, had become an acceptable modern day way of life.

The location of the Superman lab was considered to be relatively close, within commuting distance by today's standards. Yet according to yesterday's standards it would be considered a long drive out of state. Serena was just relieved that she didn't have to hop on a jet for Wisconsin this time around. Avoiding air travel felt like a big enough win in and of itself.

Serena surveyed the lab and noted that a few

things had changed. The Superman theme was still intact, brought over from the old location as per Nicholas' specifications, but his favorite superhero was now forced to share the space . Newly added décor included Tardis replicas, Daleks, and Doctor Who posters. Styluses for all the graphic tablets were in the shape of The Doctor's sonic screwdriver.

It warmed Serena's heart to know that the powers that be still had a budget and a soft spot for catering to Nicholas' tastes. Then again, as much as the government used that child, they owed him so much more- a normal childhood for starters.

"Nicholas?" Serena didn't want to startle the boy wonder who was now almost sixteen years old. He was listening to music via microchip technology. The implant was a simple procedure, as routine to the younger generations as getting piercings or tattoos. The chip was easy to program and best of all, there was no longer any need to wear ear buds. The downside to the technology, besides questions about health side effects, was that it was difficult to tell when someone was listening to music. Teachers had been working to get the chips banned, but too many students already had them, and since removing the chips required surgery, the mandate against the chips was deemed unconstitutional.

Nicholas turned around slowly, not at all surprised to see her standing there. His microchip had alerted him that someone had entered the building. It was synched with the iris reader security so he even knew exactly who it was. Besides, he was kept in the loop about such things.

Serena greeted him with, "I suppose you wonder why I'm back?"

"No, I know why you're here." Nicholas turned off his music.

"Then can you fill me in?" Serena laughed, but she was entirely serious. They were taking a stab in the dark. She didn't have the slightest idea of who to investigate first. Everyone in our government? All of the international community as well? Every world leader? Every junior staffer – everywhere? Forget the haystack, it was like finding a needle embedded in thousands of other needles, and more than one of them was tainted.

"We need to rule out some suspects to start," said Nicholas simply. Perhaps to him it really was that simple. Maybe Serena could sit back and have a cup of joe, letting Nicholas do the work.

Beav and Estep had been clearing the area to make sure that they didn't have unexpected company. They were now hovering around Nicholas' computer..

"You can sit over there," he directed. He clacked at the keyboard, preferring the keyboard over most other methods of input, even though typing was considered nearly obsolete these days.

He cued up his latest creation; software designed to eliminate wild goose chases. He called it "The Golden Egg". The program opened with a holographic animated short film that awed the three adults. A line of cartoon figures ran between and around them, much like the young jousting boys had done at the Medieval Times. The first in the line was of course the goose from the fairy tale, the one that laid golden eggs. Next in the line were all the people who had touched it and had stuck fast. The hologram weaved around and around them to a merry tune that Nicholas had composed himself, a jazzy blend of blues harmonica, piano, and even some other instrument they couldn't quite identify.

When the cartoon segment ended the program launched without further entertainment or fanfare. However, the program itself was also holographic. Nicholas said, "I didn't have your measurements so I guessed at your eye level comfort. If you want to adjust data higher or lower, nudge it with your hand."

"Awesome!" Beav slid his hologram monitor around until he reached his reading-distance preference. Estep followed suit.

Serena couldn't resist playing with her hologram, adjusting it over and over until she realized that Estep's eyes were boring into her skin. She dropped her arms down to her sides and said, "Ready when you are."

Nicholas took what looked like an Irish tin whistle from a jeweled case. He whistled a jaunty little tune, causing files to open. He stopped. "I gave you some data to browse through. This is your basic criteria for setting wild goose chase perimeters. Make your selections by touching the files. You'll be able to figure it out as you try it."

"If you say so," said Estep dubiously.

"Um, actually, don't touch anything, sir. We only need one person messing with the files." Nicholas looked from Beav to Serena. "Out of the three of you, I pick Serena."

"I'll take that as a compliment," said Serena.

Nicholas had already turned back toward his computer. He turned his personal jukebox up so loudly that they could faintly hear music coming from the chip.

"Thanks, Nicholas." Serena said, even though she knew he probably didn't hear her.

Estep grumbled, "Let's get it done. I hate this place."

Beav clapped his hands a few inches from Estep's face. "Are you in there? This is the super-secret lab of the future! We are underground, protected by top-of-the-line iris-reading security, and at this moment we are interacting with holograms floating in front of us – brand new technology that no one else knows about. We'll be the first to use it!"

"I'll be the first, only I have permission to touch the files." Serena reminded him.

Beav laughed. "Only because he declared you the lesser idiot of the two of us. Estep wasn't even considered at all."

"To quote President Kinji, his choices were Loose Cannon, Loose Screw or me."

Estep scoffed. "I assume I'm Loose Cannon."

Beav said, "I wear Loose Screw with pride."

Serena pointed at the data in front of her. "Not that I don't enjoy your self-deprecating banter but I see something already."

Estep stared at the information and then let out a ridiculously long sigh. "How long do you think this is going to take? No one's out there doing surveillance."

"Did your team leave?" Serena asked.

"Besides them."

"Are you saying that you'd rather go sit out in the car?" Serena fed him the suggestion in case he hadn't already come up with it on his own.

"Let me know when you guys find

something." Estep let himself out.

Serena turned her attention to Beav. "Look. Do you see the list in the blue folder?"

"Yes. I think we can get rid of all of that."

"All of it?"

"Why not? Postal employees, that's highly doubtful. Sanitation department. Natural resources. Parks and recreation. Libraries? Come on, Serena, we have to narrow this down and none of these agencies are likely suspects."

"Agreed." She closed the file shut by pinching it with her fingers. "What do I do now?"

"Try pressing it."

"Pressing it?"

"Tap on it." Beav demonstrated by tapping his finger on the palm of his other hand.

Serena tapped on the holographic folder and a menu popped out. She tapped on the option that said "Remove from search".

"It worked! What now?"

Beav shrugged. "I don't know."

Serena tapped on the folder again to bring up the menu she saw earlier. She tapped the option that said "Pinpoint". A flurry of hologram images burst out, scattering around the room, rotating and shuffling. The flurry was accompanied by musical chimes for every file. The sounds overlapped each other in such a jangle that it was like a porch full of wind chimes had gone off.

They waited for the files- labeled with every color in the rainbow- to stop moving and for the noise of the chimes to die down. Serena looked at Nicholas but he was buried in his work.

"Reach out and grab one of the squares," Beav suggested.

Serena snagged the next square that floated in her direction. She read it aloud "Conservative". She let go of it and it stayed in front of her. She pulled a second square from its floating space. "Lobbyist". She let it go and it snapped on top of the first square, making a stack like a virtual deck of cards. She was catching on to this.

She grabbed another and another: Pro-life, Salary $1,000,000+, Unions, Environmentalist, In Favor of One World Government, Appointed by President Ann Kinji, Senator. The next pinpoint square that floated her way caused her to do a double take: The Supporters.

Serena made an "ahah!" sound. "I understand this now. All of these descriptors can help us narrow down our list of suspects. I can make a stack of words I don't think relate to our suspects and delete them in one fell swoop."

Serena and Beav collaborated over each of the keywords. They agreed to place The Supporters onto the top of the keep stack. They tossed out words they thought were irrelevant. Keepers included words relating to foreign governments, money, powerful positions, and controversial issues.

The sleuthing pair repeated the process through fifty folders, taking up the better part of the next four hours. Finally they decided to see where they stood, even though they didn't think that they had eliminated enough suspects for the computer to generate a manageably sized list. They were stunned when the results rang up only ten names.

So engrossed in their investigation, the two barely noticed that Estep had come and gone, come and gone. Serena and Beav were still celebrating their list of ten names with whoops and high fives when Estep walked in with a tower of pizza boxes. He set the boxes on an empty work table, laid them all out and then grabbed a slice from the pie loaded with the most toppings.

Serena accepted a freshly-printed hardcopy of the list from Nicholas. "The first three on the list are the same crew that the Cube is investigating, so I suppose we leave them alone. That gives us seven remaining, four domestic and three foreign."

"Finally something concrete to work with," said Estep with his mouth full of pizza.

Serena folded the list and put it into her purse.

Beav made a *tsk, tsk* noise. "You're going to walk around with that paper on you? Did you never see a spy movie? Memorize the list and destroy it."

Serena grimaced. "My memory's not as sharp as it used to be. I'll have to make up a mnemonic trick for it. Let's see… Billy Bob and the Kangaroo went to the Bank to Cash a Check…"

"Give it to me." Estep snatched the paper

from her hands, giving Serena a paper cut in the process. He looked at the list for no longer than three seconds before running it through a paper shredder. Then he headed out the door in his usual way – no good-bye. He doubled back for one last slice, his fifth, leaving the rest of the pizza behind.

Beav said, "Once again, our cue to leave is when someone walks out." He gave Nicholas a two-fingered salute off the imaginary brim of his nonexistent hat. He stacked two boxes of pizza and carried them out.

"Thank you for your help, Nicholas. You always come through for us." Serena extended her hand and gave Nicholas' a hearty shake. "The rest of that pizza is yours. Anything left over you can give to your family, or maybe heat up for yourself. It looks like you can get a lot of meals out of it. Your parents will pick you up soon? Should we be leaving you here by yourself?"

Nicholas laughed. "Ms. Wilcox, I do this all the time. Besides, I'm not alone. There are a couple security guards on duty at all times. What did you think of Golden Egg?"

"Fully awesome. You amaze me!"

Nicholas nodded and grinned. Then he stared wistfully at her purse.

"I saw that! You're remembering that I gave you something the last time you helped us out. I haven't forgotten." Serena rummaged through her purse and pulled out something better than a pack of gum—a small retro Superman alarm clock.

Nicholas moved faster than she'd seen him move all day. He thanked her profusely and even gave her a hearty clap on the shoulder, a bit too hearty for Serena's much shorter frame.

Beav and Estep came back inside to see what the hold-up was. Serena explained, "I was saying goodbye to my good buddy."

Estep snorted. "If you gave me presents I'd be your buddy too."

Nicholas protested. "Sir, that's not why I like Ms. Wilcox."

Beav gave Estep a shove toward the open door. "Leave the kid alone. He's happy - something you wouldn't know anything about."

7

President Ann Kinji switched all incoming, and more importantly outgoing, communications to standby. She cranked up the ventilation system settings until its fans produced the obnoxiously loud mechanical whirring sound she expected. For good measure she spoke barely above a whisper. "Dr. Kendra Wellington, nice to meet you. I appreciate you flying out here on such short notice."

"Of course, Madam President. How can I be of help?" Kendra, a professor at a state university, was a young blonde married mother of a preschooler. She and her husband had tried to guess why the President of the United States requested to see her. There was nothing about Kendra that was political, except for having recently taught a 100-level political science course. The course had been dumped on her lap when the university couldn't find a substitute for a professor out on maternity leave.

Ann gestured for Kendra to come closer. She rasped, "I want to understand the authority of the UN."

Kendra dropped her voice to match the president's whisper. "What do you mean by 'authority'?" Kendra realized that she had been right—President Kinji wanted Kendra for her expertise. Kendra hoped she knew the answers; she had taught at the general elective level, and she wasn't sure how much of the curriculum she even remembered.

"Specifically, I want to know if I can make a direct appeal to the UN to give me the power to circumvent the House and the Senate. I am seeking a total bypass of the two governmental branches, making me temporarily Queen or, in a less kind but perhaps more accurate view, Dictator of the United States of America."

Kendra's eyes widened but she kept her composure. She hesitated for only a second or two before whispering, "To say that I'm speechless is an understatement. Please forgive me if it takes me a few minutes to formulate my response."

Ann dropped the whispering, but still spoke quietly. "I understand." She watched Kendra's face as the young woman's mind raced. When she saw that Kendra was visibly more relaxed she said, "Are you composed now?"

"I'm as composed as I'll ever be." Kendra said.

"Good. Before we begin I prefer, and even require, that my intentions be clear from the start. I'm recording our conversation and I ask you to pay close attention to every word that passes from my lips."

Ann spoke directly into the microphone source. "My intention is to take over the United States government on a temporary basis not to exceed six months, in a temporary measure to gain control over rampant government corruption that is an immediate and direct threat to not only our nation, but to the world."

Kendra suppressed the urge to gasp. She formulated what she thought was a responsible question. "What will you do with your temporary circumvention of checks and balances?"

"Investigate every member of the House and Senate."

"I don't understand why you need the UN to give you sole authority for this purpose. You can investigate openly, you already have that authority." Kendra's eyes flitted about the room as if hoping that someone else would emerge who could take her place.

Ann shook her head with enough force that her signature onyx bob trembled. "No, I don't have authority to investigate as thoroughly as required. I want to restrict Internet access for all Americans and convince world leaders to limit Internet access abroad as well. That alone is a move that Congress will never agree to."

"That objective seems impossible. What basis do you have for believing you can accomplish Internet restriction?" As soon as the words left her lips Kendra regretted them. How could she be so bold as to challenge President Ann Kinji?

If Ann was offended she didn't show it. "I have access to people who know these things. They assure me that it's possible. Eventually hackers will find a way around the restrictions, but even a day or two of blocked communications will be of great help to us."

"Cell phones?"

"Now you are catching on. Yes, I want to block *all* communications. The powers behind the layers of conspiracy and treason are geographically spread out, of that I am certain. If we cut them off from each other, they will be forced to meet in person."

"Or wait it out? They may be patient."

"They know that I'm closing in on them. I predict that they will react by connecting with each other. However, it doesn't really matter which way they respond. If they think they can wait it out, I'll benefit from that as well."

"How so?"

"Whatever it is that they are planning, they will be thrown off course. It gives my team time to find them before they take another step. They have been blocking, tracking and censoring Internet communications for years. I feel strongly that shutting things down on their end is going to throw them for a loop. Regardless, that's only a small part of what I would do with full authority over Congress. Can it be done? Does the UN have the authority to grant me my emergency petition?"

The phrase 'emergency petition' jogged her memory; Kendra now understood why President Kinji had requested her. She had invited her political science students to join in class discussion online but the only person who visited the forum was a foreign exchange student who enjoyed debate. He and Kendra had a rather lengthy dialog about the history of the UN that was entirely public—how could she have forgotten this? Anyone searching for active scholarly discussions about the UN could easily find it. Yes, that had to be it.

Confident that she understood her purpose for being here, Kendra slipped into her comfortable role of teacher. "You might recall that the UN got a toehold into a one-world government of sorts when the child disability act was passed. That bill gave the UN the authority to regulate, or legislate, over our own laws. Since then, the UN has passed several similar acts, all of it leading to this situation. Yes, President Kinji, the UN most certainly can give you authority over the United States, superseding our own laws-- assuming that you can convince them to grant it to you. You are proposing a temporary emergency measure, and it's possible they will be agreeable to it, but you'll have to make a strong case for its necessity. Do you have friends at the UN?"

"Friends, enemies, and frenemies."

"I don't like your chances, but yes, they have the power to give you what you want."

"Thank you for your time. That's all I needed to know."

"If you don't mind my asking, I'd like permission to stay on." Kendra couldn't believe she was daring to ask, but she'd never forgive herself if she didn't try.

"To stay on?"

"May I be an observer, a historian? I won't speak without your permission. My role is only that of a witness."

"I welcome your involvement. And you don't need to sit by in silence. Speak freely; I value your input."

Kendra took a deep breath. Should she dare say what's on her heart? "I do have a few thoughts I'd like to share with you right now, actually."

"Fire away."

"Obviously the UN had a major role in the rebuilding of the United States post Big War, otherwise known as World War 3 everywhere else but in our own country."

"We don't call it World War 3 because few nations other than our own were involved. It was a limited engagement, catastrophic as it was. We took care of it quickly, involving few."

"Ah, but that's far from the truth. The economic collapse affected everyone."

"The collapse was averted."

"That's my point. It was averted because the UN stepped in with the Global Initiative, the first of its kind. Of course the Global Initiative spidered into the Global Oil Initiative and several others, but the Global Initiative covers it all. Anyway, that's how all of this began, this corruption that you are addressing now. The desperation of the United States created a window of opportunity for the loan sharks of the world to jump through."

"Loan sharks? I haven't heard the global investors referred to that way before, yet I suppose I'd be hard pressed to find a more accurate description."

Kendra leaned forward and clasped her hand over the microphone sensor. She whispered as quietly as her voice could drop. "The sharks are calling in the loan."

Ann studied Kendra's face and after seeing fear in her eyes, she allowed her hand to remain over the microphone sensor. She followed suit and lowered her voice as well. "That's all out in the open. We all know that the United States is squeezed. We are loaning our military to all manner of global situations, all gratis, to pay down on our debts. We are also gifting food and other resources. We are making good on our word, on our agreement with the UN."

Kendra looked wildly about the room, this time worried that someone really would appear.

"No, that's not what I'm talking about. The above-board loans are being paid as per the terms of the contracts signed by yourself and President John Williams. No one disputes that."

"What are you implying?"

Kendra hesitated. "I can't imagine that you aren't aware of the other loans."

Ann switched off the microphone. "Other loans?"

Kendra's arm ached from covering the microphone sensor for so long, funny how she hadn't felt the strain on her muscles until now. All of her sensations were off kilter. The confidence she felt a few minutes ago was gone. "The secret deals, the hand-shakes under the table."

President Ann was speechless. She was a statue, blinking at Kendra.

"You didn't know?" Kendra searched about the room, her longing to be replaced by someone else had intensified. And yet, she wanted to stay.

"Do you have any proof? How and what do you know about this?" Ann put Kendra on the spot even though she knew that her statements held an undeniable ring of truth.

"Well, I thought it was common knowledge. It's been rather out in the open. Don't you keep track of what's on the social media channel?" Kendra was proud of herself for not only staying in the room but for holding her own in the conversation as well.

"We track various keywords, yes. I don't understand how we could have missed something like this." Ann paced the length of the room, a large room the size of Kendra's entire modest floor space at her house, a home that felt far away from her at the moment.

Kendra rallied her thoughts and ventured, "They could have been cloaking themselves."

"Cloaking?" Ann was near Kendra's ear, rasping again.

Kendra again lowered her voice. "The Internet sources I'm talking about might have blocks on their content and their addresses so that you can't track them. But even so, why hasn't anyone brought it to your attention? Surely people have discovered it for themselves just by using the Internet on their own."

"I don't know how to answer that."

Kendra didn't know what to say either.

"Spies and patriots alike have been cloaking and blocking, censoring and hacking; both officially and unofficially. I don't see how we can control the anarchy that is the Internet. The only way to regain any sort of order is to shut it down." Ann threw her hands up in a flourish that sent her bob in motion, her turned-up locks swinging like a pendulum. She paced back and forth for several minutes, her head bent and her hands formed into fists. Finally she meandered back over to Kendra and looked at her expectantly.

Kendra had been digging into her purse for her phone while Ann was pacing. She held her phone out to her now. "Here, let me show you. It's easy to find layperson and expert forums about what I'm talking about."

"No, I'll do you one better. Wave your hand in front of the hologram."

Kendra's eyes lit up. "I've seen one of these before, but I've never used one. How do I do a search?"

"Talk to the hologram as if it was a real person. I call her Sally."

Kendra begged her mind to remember this

moment always—she would be retelling this at dinner parties for the rest of her life. "Sally, please do a search for all articles relating to 'loan shark global deals'."

Forty-four results came up on the projection screen. As the two women browsed through the list, selected articles, and began to skim them, a red light flashed over the screen. It blinked without ceasing until Ann picked up her phone. The phone looked surprisingly vintage and appeared to be hardwired to the wall. "Nicholas, is this you?"

"Yes, it's me, President Kinji."

"If you are calling me on this line this can't be good."

"No, it isn't. I got a trigger."

"A trigger?"

"Your search kicked off a trigger. Someone was tracking your keywords, you know, like we do. Except this isn't one of ours. This trace is foreign."

"Foreign meaning not of our department?"

"No, foreign meaning not of our country."

"Which country?"

"I don't know. I'm working on it."

"Thank you Nicholas. Do you need more hands to sort this out?"

"I have the team you gave me. That's enough. But you better stop whatever it is that you are doing. Let me do it here."

"I already got what I need. If I need anything else, I'll let you know." Ann disconnected the contact with Nicholas and turned her attention back to Kendra. "All of these results are from fringe groups or extremists, not 'everywhere' as you've asserted."

Kendra blushed. "These are popular sources that have become mainstream. Like this one, The Supporters, they are especially good."

"The Supporters? That's one I'm familiar with. We're dealing with them right now."

"You should have been aware of this information. It's out there, in a big enough way that it's hard to imagine you not knowing about it. Who's in charge of the keyword traces you talked about? That person is either really bad at their job or deliberately hiding the information from you."

"The Cube is a vacuum. It's easy to be kept in the dark, even more so if someone wants it that way. Skip Sally, show me on your phone."

Kendra used a hotkey to call up a previous search. Nothing happened. She manually typed the search keywords into her phone. The search results were completely unrelated to her keywords. "I don't understand. How can this be? My presets are wiped clean and my searches are blocked. But my phone has never left my purse!"

Ann fumed, "Now we know why I didn't know about the so-called loan shark global deals- my entire office is hacked!"

8

"The president is in trouble," said Nicholas.

"Yes, I assumed that when the alarm sounded. I know I'm not a genius like you, but I'm further up the chain than a monkey," said Estep.

"Hey, easy. You're more snarly than your usual endearing self. Did your girlfriend dump you?" Beav stepped in.

Beav's girlfriend references and jabs were nothing more than barbs; Beav knew nothing of

Estep's private life. Yet Estep visibly flinched as if slapped in the face.

"Oh, wow, hey man I'm sorry." Beav clapped him on the back. "Still no reason to take it out on the kid."

"Which girlfriend? Katalina?" Serena realized as soon as the words left her lips that she should have kept her nose out of it. Serena didn't know much about Estep's private life either, but she overheard enough on-the-road phone conversations to know more than he would have liked for her to have.

But if Estep assumed that Serena enjoyed hearing about the gossipy details of other people's romantic encounters, he was wrong. Serena made a practice of avoiding such conversations. What could she do if she was stuck in the passenger's seat while Estep was having a loud personal conversation on the road?

"She said it's between her and the job."

"And you chose the job." Serena stated the obvious.

Estep stormed out of the room.

"That's your reaction to everything!"

Beav shut the door behind him. "Let him go.

He's been fairly useless anyway."

The two contemplated how useless Estep was until Nicholas interrupted their thoughts. His voice sounded like he had been crying. "Please! I don't know what to do. I can't remove the blocks. I don't have their technology."

"Whose technology? What technology?" asked Beav.

Nicholas answered, "I don't know who is behind this. It's Japanese technology. People get paranoid about information being shared or sold, privacy violations, and all of that. This is worse. It's information *prevented* from being shared."

Beav said, "I'm not sure I follow."

Serena explained, "Our words are blocked, controlled, and denied free speech. Who knows how long this has been going on."

Nicholas' face was pale. "Ms. Wilcox, they have the Internet and there's nothing I can do to get it back. President Kinji's office is hacked. She can't use any device to connect to the Internet without hacker interference and spies tracking her every move."

"This isn't all on you." Beav ran his hands through his hair. "Crikey, this is too much for a kid to take on." His face reddened, not an easy feat given his olive skin tone.

"It's better than prison," said Nicholas.

"Prison? Why would you ever have to worry about prison?" Serena smiled. She assumed that Nicholas was being dramatic.

"That's where kids like me are going. It's called 'Proactive imprisonment'. They send us to the criminally insane youth house. That's what happened to some of the kids in my Mensa group. The only reason why I'm not on the list is because I work for the government. If I lose my job they'll put me on the list. I have to fix this!"

"Whoa, slow down. Tell us what's going on." Beav sat down and rolled his chair next to Nicholas.

Nicholas shrugged, a movement barely perceptible given his slumped shoulders. "People are afraid of kids like me after all that's happened. You know, with mass murder-suicides in schools, theaters, malls..."

Serena lunged forward and gave Nicholas a hug. "Just look at this computer lab with your favorite heroes all around you. They built this lab for you because you are one of the good guys. No one's putting you on a list."

Nicholas brightened up instantly, and even grinned. "But I can't trust your judgment, Ms. Wilcox. You *like* crazy people."

"You mean this guy here?" Serena jabbed her thumb toward Beav.

"No, I mean Paul Tracy and the others in the criminally insane ward. You're always asking me to get Paul online for you to talk to him."

"You're right, Nicholas. I like crazy. Not the criminal part, obviously, but this gives me an idea. The imprisoned haven't been cut off from talking to each other, correct? Last I knew, they had older technology, nothing but time on their hands, and still had freedom of information."

Nicholas agreed. "Right. There's no blocking software on their obsolete systems. Prisons, nursing homes, and even some schools haven't gotten the upgrade yet. They don't access the Internet the same way that private citizens or government employees do. But if you want to use their systems you have to go to where they are. I can't do it from here. What I can do is use their outdated software to make a patch to fix this blocking hack. Thanks for the idea Ms.

Wilcox."

Serena shook her head. "No, no, I can't take credit for that. But before you get lost in that project, could you set something up for me? I don't want computer connections – I want people, real face-to-face communication. I want to assemble a think tank of people who have been in the loop on every conspiracy theory, every overheard half-baked half-truth and every resource for propaganda that every good extremist should know."

Beav laughed, "Those whack-jobs are *responsible* for most of those conspiracy theories!"

"Maybe so, but they get their ideas from things they've seen and heard. The best fiction begins with a kernel of truth. I want to sort the fact from the fiction and dig through the layers of paranoid delusion until I hit that kernel."

"And then?" Beav pressed.

"I'll trace it back to where it came from and voila! We'll have something to go on." Serena pulled an elastic ponytail holder from the outer pocket of her small travel purse and swept her long dark hair back away from her face.

"It's as easy as that?" Beav shook his head.

"Agent Estep's negativity is wearing off on you." Serena clucked her tongue.

"We can't let that happen – I must resist! Count me in." Beav pointed at Serena's ponytail. "I see you're ready for action."

Nicholas offered, "I can send for them so you don't have to go back to the prison."

Beav questioned, "Wouldn't that take a lot of red tape and time we don't have?"

"I have a fast-track. President Kinji gave me an emergency pass for anything you ask for. Well, I mean, anything official you ask for. I don't think it works on pizza delivery or something like that." Nicholas said all of this without any hint that he understood how powerful he was, this child who didn't even have a driver's license yet.

Serena clasped her hands together. "Wonderful! I want all the members of the criminally insane club: Paul, Victor, Lita and Vanessa. And I assume that their transport includes armed guards who will stay with them?"

"Yes." Nicholas hesitated and then added,

"Can I ask you to add my friend? He's not insane and he didn't do anything wrong. He could help."

"You mentioned earlier that you and your friends are profiled and some are added to a list. I don't understand – enlighten me," Serena prodded.

Nicholas paused only a short while before filling them in. "There's a watch list we aren't supposed to know about, and high IQ kids are on it. The government monitors our Internet usage and school records for any sign of fitting the profile for violence, like if we are taking any prescription drugs, or if we are bullied in school. And if any of us say things against the government, we get put on two lists that are cross referenced. My friend was on the potential mass murderer list and the terrorist watch list. When he got on the first list he was pulled in and questioned. After he was put on the second list he was arrested."

"How did he fit the profile for violence, besides his IQ?" asked Serena.

"He had few friends, he kept to himself, he was quiet, and he didn't join in – he was rated as an outsider and loner."

"Rated? What do you mean rated?" Serena asked.

"Oh, it's routine. They do the ratings at the end of fall term every year. There's a scale of 1-5 on criteria like 'joins in on social activities'. They rated him a 1. He didn't join in, but that's only because his friends don't go to his school. I'm one of his best friends and I'm homeschooled, so no one in his class ever saw me. Besides, the social activities were stupid. He didn't want to go. But he's not a loner, Ms. Wilcox. Another thing: he was bullied, so he got 5 points deducted from his score."

"Who's doing these ratings?" Serena struggled not to let her horror show.

"Classmates, teachers…" Nicholas said distractedly. He was typing in the forms to arrange for the criminally insane crew to be transported from the prison to the Superman lab.

Beav, who had been listening to the conversation and had been simmering on slow boil, could bear it no longer. Pounding his fist into his hand to punctuate his sentences, he jumped onto his soapbox.

"The *victim* of bullying is the one persecuted and prosecuted? Rather than resolving the bullying problems, they proactively arrest victims who might snap? Nice touch that Big Brother wraps it all under the terrorism umbrella. As of 2012, the American government has the authority to indefinitely retain anyone suspected of ties to terrorism. In recent years the definition for what acts can be considered acts of terrorism has broadened. I knew it, I knew it would lead to something insane. I see now it's come down to arresting people –kids! - before they even do anything wrong!"

Serena stood between Nicholas and Beav, putting one hand on each of their shoulders. "I know it's not likely that I'm the one to get us back on topic, seeing how it's me who got us off topic, but we need to plow through. Yes, Nicholas, bring your friend in too."

Nicholas spun around to face his computer. He hit the send button on the prison transport request form. "Done."

"I need a few others for the Think Tank," said Serena, just as the form went through.

"More prisoners?" asked Nicholas,

despairing at the thought of entering another form.

"No. I want the Supporters brought in."

"The Supporters? I don't think I can do that. I can't hack them. They do things old school. I heard they even use carrier pigeons, but that's probably a hoax."

Serena laughed. "Relax. I don't know about the pigeons, but I do know how to get a hold of them."

"How?" asked Beav.

"Like this." Serena took her phone out of her purse and punched in a number. "It's Serena, can we meet?" She paused to listen. "Yes, at the lab." To Nicholas and Beav she said, "They'll be here within the hour."

"You weren't supposed to tell anyone about the lab!" Nicholas yelped.

"I didn't have to, they already know."

Beav gestured for Serena to follow him to the conference table area. "We need to talk. One day The Supporters are kidnapping you and your family and the next day you're old friends."

Serena stayed where she was, planted next to Nicholas' computer. "I'll catch you up to speed later. I need Nicholas to send out one more invitation first."

9

To say that Joseph Smythe found Serena's invitation unexpected was an understatement. What could it all mean? And a secret meeting at a secret government computer lab? He was truly living in a different world. No longer an ordinary politician, he was being drafted as a sidekick, assigned to either a superhero or a villain, and he had no idea which way the casting would go. It was a disappointment then when a perfectly drab government sedan was his transport.

"Is someone going to explain to me why I've been recruited for this Think Tank project?" Joseph Smythe asked the driver.

The driver was a personal friend of the President and the First Gentleman. Penny had been an official Cube driver for years, but had moved on when she graduated from law school. She was more than willing to get back behind the wheel upon special request for Operation Bluebird Flown. The sedan was not registered with The Cube, so even if someone looked into where the Speaker of the House was off to, there would be no record of it. Nothing but the video footage of the pick-up. To be sure that she wouldn't be identified, Penny had worn a disguise – she was made up to look like a man, which was why Smythe was calling her Kevin, the name on her uniform tag.

"Seriously, Kevin, as Speaker of the House I have clearance way beyond your pay grade. So tell me, where is this Superman lab?"

"Sorry, Mr. Speaker, I can't divulge that information," said Penny, knowing that the cat was out of the bag as soon as she spoke.

"You're a woman! I suppose I can stop calling you Kevin now. Tell me what the Sam Hill is going on!"

"You do know that President Kinji is investigating everyone."

"Yes, I'm aware. And she can do that right here. There's no need to send me off to Siberia."

"Calm down. The lab is not far. Depending on traffic flow, we could be there by dinner time."

"That eases my mind some. Tell me, Kevin, what's your real name?"

"Penny."

"And you're dressed like a man because you were tricking the surveillance cameras?"

"Correct."

"Is someone demanding a ransom for my safe return?"

"You haven't been kidnapped."

"A joke, a joke. I'm not upset. I rather like a good adventure."

Penny looked into the mirror to see Smythe's affable grin. "I'm glad you see it that way."

Smythe's nearly six foot frame was beginning to cramp up in his backseat position.

His nickname "Beanpole" was apt, but the older he got the less flexible he was. Travel was a killer. "You say we'll be there soon?"

Penny had a lot of experience volunteering her time to youth activities. She used her best patient-adult voice when she said, "Mr. Speaker, why don't you listen to an audio book? There's a full library at your disposal."

Smythe got the point and left Penny alone for a good hour before he tried again. "You really won't tell me what to expect? Can you at least tell me if I'm on the winning team on this thing? This isn't an interrogation I've foolishly agreed to is it?" Smythe's love of adventure had its limits.

Penny turned onto a gravel road. "We're here, Mr. Speaker. You can ask them yourself."

10

Serena, Beav and Nicholas made party preparations for the Think Tank session. Nicholas showed them to a small lounge area, but that space was entirely too intimate. This group required a lot of personal space. The OCD guests would be quickly agitated if their personal space bubbles weren't respected.

The conference table area was the only viable option, but the table was too small to accommodate all of their guests. The three of them moved the table and set it in the back of the lab. They then wheeled dozens of computer chairs from the various stations, the conference table chairs, and even a few stacking chairs they found in a storage closet, and situated the chairs around the perimeter of the conference area. They closed their rectangular group "circle" in on one side at the back wall of the lab, in front of the table. The other side was closed in by cutting across the width of the lab, just before the computer stations. By using the entire conference area section they now had enough room for the Think Tank to sit with enough personal space for no touching.

Beav reflected on their work and remarked, "We'll need to give them water."

Nicholas remembered seeing a shockingly large surplus of foam coffee cups with plastic lids in the storage closet. No one had used them from the previous top-secret government labs over the years – disposable foam cups were no longer sold, after the EPA modernized the Toxic Substances Control Act, banning hundreds of products that were previously used daily by millions of people.

The banning of foam cups stemmed from a 2001 Department of Health and Human Services report that classified styrene, which is used in the manufacture of polystyrene, as "reasonably anticipated to be a human carcinogen." Somehow the lab had acquired boxes and boxes of foam cups. Nicholas retrieved one of those boxes now and the three of them spent the next fifteen minutes filling twenty-five cups with water. They placed one cup of water on the floor beside every chair.

"I think we're done here. We don't need party favors." Beav clapped his hands loudly, a sound that echoed in the nearly empty lab.

"Are you set up to record everything that goes on?" Serena directed the question to Nicholas.

"Everything that happens here is always recorded." Nicholas pointed to the various cameras positioned so that not one inch of the lab wasn't under constant steady surveillance.

"Beyond security camera footage – I need high resolution video with clear sound." Serena thought she was clarifying her point, but Nicholas was way ahead of her.

"Ms. Wilcox, all of the cameras in the lab are state of the art. In 'movie mode', which I already selected for you, the image quality is cinema grade."

"Ah, well, my apologies. I see you were already on it." Serena surveyed the room and found nothing else left to consider, nothing but how on Earth she was going to conduct a meeting comprised of criminally insane persons, a band of vigilantes and the Speaker of the House. She didn't have much time for musing. The first round of party guests entered the lab: The Supporters.

Nicholas had lost interest in the whole affair. He stayed at the lab in case he was needed, but he was released from duty and was already plugged into his ear chip sound station while simultaneously programming a high tech computer game he was creating in a joint project with other NASA I.N.S.P.I.R.E students. While Serena, always the mother, worried about Nicholas' exposure to potentially dangerous situations, she was reassured that he was checked out of the whole experience and was unlikely to hear a word they were saying.

Beav, however, was keenly interested and had no intention of missing a single second of the absurd Think Tank session about to commence. He could hardly wait to meet The Supporters and was completely thrown when he recognized not one, but two of the faces that came through the lab doors.

"We meet again," said Bob, the radio host Beav met in the rural Indiana farmhouse.

"Surprised to see you here, Bob, but not as surprised as I am to see *you*." Beav bowed in an exaggerated gesture of respect.

Standing before him was mentalist Eric Dittelman, whose career began after becoming a semi-finalist on the 2011 season of the classic talent show "America's Got Talent", which had made household names out of hundreds of previously unknown talents. Dittelman had gone on to tour and fame of his own right. What was his connection to The Supporters? What could this be about? Beav peered behind Dittelman to Serena, hoping she would end his curiosity.

Serena shrugged.

Bob ended the suspense. "I see you know who Eric Dittelman is. He's not one of us, so you can stop looking at him like he's an alien from another planet, which do exist by the way, I have on good authority. Anyway, he came to us with a tip. He's a concerned citizen and a good guy – that's as far as it goes. He was kind enough to agree to come with us today to explain his observation in person."

"Wonderful! Thank you, Mr. Dittelman, honored to have you." Serena stepped into the gaggle of Supporters. Her not-quite-five-two frame was quickly swallowed up by the swarm. She extended her hand to shake Dittelman's.

Dittelman flashed his signature grin, a smile like that of a Yellow Lab – too friendly for guile, too honest for treachery. The instant trust established, Dittelman's words would carry a lot of weight. Serena hoped whatever he had to say was full of helpful details.

Bob, having been the only person to have met Beav, had taken it upon himself to introduce the others. "This is Joanna Murphy from Ireland…"

A beautiful woman with porcelain skin and carroty red tresses stepped forward. Her eyes were the same shade of green as Serena's.

Serena blurted, "My grandmother's maiden name was Murphy."

Joanna said, "Murphy is a common Irish surname, about 50,000 or so in Ireland alone. I doubt we're cousins. Call me Jo, by the way."

Serena complied. "Jo, why is someone from Ireland get involved with The Supporters?"

"I'm not presently living in Ireland. I'm a surgeon at the Mayo Clinic in Minnesota. Besides, America's problems are world problems."

Bob nodded. "Jo has been a huge asset to our group. The rest of our gang, as you can see, are all men. He pointed at each man as he said his name. "Devin, Craig, Dennis, Mahesh, Kobin, Garreth, Tristan, and Luke." Bob addressed Beav. "Luke Halloway is who you were talking to over the airwaves in my studio."

"You're much younger than what I imagined," said Beav.

Luke grimaced. "I haven't heard that before."

Serena ignored Luke's dripping sarcasm. "So there are ten of you, plus your guest star Eric Dittelman? Or are there more of you at home?"

"Oh you have no idea how funny that is,"

said Luke.

Jo added, "We wouldn't fit in here if we all turned up, in fact, we could fill up an entire city. We have a massive Internet presence. But, if you want to count only those of us who meet in person, we have about 300 active members in our chapter, and there are over a dozen chapters across the nation. I'd say we have about 5,000 members who meet on a weekly basis. The rest are Internet-only, but the numbers are staggering and growing by the hour."

"I'm afraid I'll have a hard time remembering all of your names," said Serena.

Jo dismissed her concern. "Oh, don't worry about that. Remember us three: Luke, Bob and me. Luke is the founder and head of all, Bob is our communications director and I'm a glorified secretary. If you need any archives, and we do record everything we do, come to me. If you need to get in touch with Luke, contact Bob. The rest of the group does the behind-the-scenes work. It takes five of them to handle the tech support for the Internet chapters."

Serena asked, "Luke, why do we have to contact you through Bob?"

Luke didn't respond.

Serena caught on that he was listening to music—he had an ear chip like Nicholas'. She tried again, louder. "Luke!"

Luke looked at her.

"Why do we have to contact you through Bob? Don't you have a way we can reach you directly?"

Luke said, "Few people have my contact information. I'm careful that way."

Beav said, "I'm confused. I thought Serena had already met your group – isn't that what that whole in-the-corn thing was about? Wasn't she with you?"

Serena explained, "I didn't meet anyone from the head organization. A committee from the Indiana chapter met me in the corn."

Their conversation came to an abrupt halt when they heard the lab doors open. Agent Estep, who had been kept in the loop, was not about to miss out on the Think Tank farce. If his career was going down the toilet, he had to at least give it a proper farewell. He entered the lab and strode directly to where Serena was standing.

Serena made generalized introductions and then led the group to the Think Tank rectangle. "Please sit together as a group. Our other guests will be accompanied by armed escorts."

Guffaws, murmurs and chuckles went up. All seemed game for whatever was about to happen. "Who else is coming? Criminals?"

The lab doors reopened and the Speaker of the House entered. "I wouldn't call myself a criminal."

The Supporters stood and a hush came over the room. Joseph Smythe, extended to his full lanky height, wearing a dapper wool blend brown herringbone fedora hat, a brown velvet sport coat blazer, slacks, a white dress shirt, a yellow tie, and brown loafers, looked like he walked right off the set of a classic Hollywood movie – before color film. His attire should have come off as outlandish, but he pulled it off with his boyish charm. Unlike Carson and his ilk, Smythe was genuine, with kind eyes. Or so the only two women in the room thought.

Serena, who had programmed her brain to never see another man as anything other than "somebody's son or brother" when she got married, was not smitten. However, Jo was practically swooning. Jo quickly collected herself enough to initiate conversation. She stepped forward with outstretched hand. "What brings you to Serena's Think Tank today, Mr. Speaker?"

"Call me Joe. And you are?"

Joanna blushed. "Also Jo."

Joe laughed. He looked expectant.

"Without the E, short for Joanna. Joanna Murphy."

"Oh! You really are named Jo. Good fun in that, Joe and Jo." He smiled broadly.

Jo's face revealed how much she liked the sound of that.

Spellbound by the awkwardness of spying on this magical moment when dapper politician meets pretty Irish activist, everyone else stood frozen. Estep broke the spell by clearing his throat. He offered his own hand to shake and gestured for Mr. Speaker, or Joe as he had so casually renamed himself, to take a seat. There was a brief pause and a mournful expression that flitted over Joe's face as he realized that the seats on both sides of where Jo was sitting were already taken.

Joe settled in between Serena and Estep, which was a good idea since the pair of them were better off separated from each other.

"I'd like to wait until the others arrive before we get started. Oh, I think that's them now," said Serena.

There was a clatter of chairs as the newcomers seated themselves. The group was now situated in the rectangle and the twenty – five chairs were all occupied. Along the back wall area were the nine who came from the adult prison system: Paul, Victor, Lita and Vanessa, and their four armed escorts. They were seated with a guard between each of them. Along the opposite side, in the row of chairs that were in the middle of the room, where the flooring changed over from the commercial carpeting in the computer lab area to the tile under their feet in the conference area, were Eric Dittelman, Beav, Serena, Speaker of the House Joe, and Estep.

Along the sides of the rectangle was everyone else. The Supporters in key roles positioned themselves close to the middle of the room where Serena and company were seated. Luke and Jo were on the side nearest to Dittelman. Bob was on the side nearest to Estep. On Bob's left was Nicholas' friend and his youth prison escort. The remaining Supporters filled in the rest of the seats.

"Let me make a few introductions before we get started." Serena grabbed a notepad from her purse and referred to it as she spoke. "Beginning on my left, going down the row along the left hand wall, we have a young man named Marco…"

"Polo!" shouted several people.

Serena waited for the giggles to die down. She wasn't used to such a lively bunch. "Marco was arrested because he was on a terrorist watch list. We don't believe that he's done anything wrong, and his insights could be useful to us. Next to him is his armed escort. Along both sides of the room are members of The Supporters. Along the back wall are prisoners from the adult criminally insane facility who need no introduction since all are now infamous."

"In my own row here," Serena gestured

toward herself and the others seated near her. She continued to gesture as she named each person. "We have celebrity Eric Dittelman who is here because he has something important to share, and on my immediate right is Beav, which is fitting because he's my right hand man in this investigation. Next to me on my left is, as you know, Mr. Speaker of the House Joseph Smythe – or Joe, as he has requested we call him. And on the other side of Joe is Agent Estep who is our official chain of command to President Kinji."

"If I still have a job," Estep said under his breath in a stage whisper that could be heard all the way across the room.

Serena was distracted by his grumbling for only a second. "Let's begin. What I want to hear is every conspiracy theory you know of, anything you've heard through the grapevine, anything you've come up with yourself, and most of all, anything you have proof of." The room immediately erupted in an impressive din of overlapping voices. "Wait, wait!"

Estep stood up and put his two fingers into his mouth. He whistled at a pitch that instantly silenced the room. He sat back down and threw his arms toward Serena in a "giving it back to you" gesture.

"Thank you, Agent Estep. Instead of a free-for-all, we have to do this one person at a time. Show of hands, who has actual proof to back up your theory?"

Serena, Beav and Estep gaped slack-jawed as every hand in the room was raised except for their own. The prisoners, the escorts, The Supporters, Eric Dittelman, and even Speaker of the House Joe – all had their hands raised.

11

Former Special Agent Lehman, recalled by President Kinji back into service, was now an emergency Vice Presidential appointment. His professional life after he left the civil service was fulfilling. He never once looked back. And yet, when the president called, he didn't even need to think it over – when his wife agreed he should go, he packed his bags. But things had gotten out of control. How did he go from enjoying GianMarco's Veal Osso Bucco to catching a cafeteria meal at The Cube? Sure, he could get anything he wanted ordered up, but somehow everything ended up tasting the same.

Meanwhile in his absence his wife had gotten a new job in Texas and that's where the two of them lived now – except that he wasn't living there. He was still here, living in a governmental suite on the outer perimeter of The Cube. What choice did he have really? Of course he would answer the call. He went to the hologram room to talk to his wife. She always got him refocused. He passed through the eye scan, recited his Texan address for the house he had only seen through pictures, and waited only a second or two before his wife appeared on the platform in front of him.

They talked about the learning curve at her new job and she asked him how he was coping with the stress of the investigation, that all of America knew about to some degree. He was about to say something when he felt someone's presence. His wife's face morphed into a mask of horror was the last thing Lehman saw before everything went dark.

When he came to, the first thing he saw was

his wife's face peering at him from above. But how? How could the hologram image shift like that?

"Can you hear me?"

Lehman tried to answer but his tongue was too heavy in his mouth. Nothing came out but gibberish. It was enough.

"He's awake! He's awake!" Lehman's wife signaled for a nurse. Before long the entire ward filed into the room. It wasn't every day that the Vice President of the United States was their number one patient.

"You had a nasty hit to the head," said one of the doctors. Lehman tried to sort out what they were saying to him while his head was still too fuzzy to keep up. He motioned for all of them to stop talking. Then he fell asleep.

When he woke, he was started to see not his wife's face looking down at him but President Kinji's instead. "Good to see you are coming around," she said.

Lehman mumbled something incoherent. He groaned and tried again. This time he managed to rasp out an intelligible sentence. "I'm sorry."

"Sorry for what? You didn't do anything

wrong." Ann's eyes were soft and compassionate.

"I'm out of service," he croaked.

"Only temporarily. You're going to be just fine. But we need to find out who did this to you, and why? What purpose did it serve to knock you out like that?" Ann pondered the question and came up with nothing.

Lehman drifted in and out of sleep for the next ten minutes. Ann had planned to stay no more than fifteen minutes and was on her way out when he suddenly sat up in bed.

His heart racing and his mind clear, he reached out to grab Ann's sleeve. She strained her ears to hear his whisper. "They took my eyes, they took my eyes."

"Your eyes? What do you mean?" Ann hovered over the nurses' station sensor. She paused to give him a chance to give her a reasonable explanation, hesitation that proved wise.

Lehman took a few sips of water before attempting to speak. "They carried me. I remember. Where did you find me?"

"In the Gallery."

"Outside the Northwest wing?" Lehman attempted to clear his throat but his throat was so sore and raw that tears sprang to his eyes.

"Yes."

"Top secret clearance to enter wing." He was fading fast. He was losing his fight against the powerful sedatives coursing through his veins.

"Iris scanner!" It made sense to her now.

Before surrendering to a deep undisturbed sleep he said, "Yes. They needed my eyes."

Ann squeezed Lehman's hand, thanked his wife, and left the hospital with her security detail flanking her. She was on the phone with Nicholas as soon as she was in route to The Cube. "Hey, kiddo, we have another complication."

"I'm sorry to hear that President Kinji. How can I help?"

"I can hear you. You don't need to shout."

"Oops, sorry, I had my ear chip on," said Nicholas, his voice now at the correct volume.

"I need you to examine footage from The Cube. I need to know Vice President Lehman's every move for the past 24 hours."

"Hold on. It will only take a couple of

minutes." Nicholas' fingers scurried across the keyboard like a vial of spiders on the loose. His keyboarding skills were not only self-taught, but he had somehow invented his own bizarre technique in the process. Both hands moved across the keyboard in sweeping patterns that resembled the movements of an accomplished pianist. If Ann was able to watch him she would have been mesmerized. "Got it."

"What does that mean? You have the footage or you found something?" Ann was still in route, now at a stop-and-go choke point. She had some time, but not much. She wanted to finish their conversation before returning to The Cube, where the walls had ears.

"Yes."

"Yes what? You found something or you have the footage?"

"Both."

"Archive the footage…"

"Already did."

"And tell me what you found."

"One guy hit Lehman from behind. Then two more guys came up and grabbed him under the arms. The guy who hit him got in front of him and there was another guy just sort of standing around. And two more guys in the back."

"You're losing me. There were six men?"

"Yes, six. They huddled around him in a pack so they could drag him off without anyone noticing." Nicholas hit a few keys. "I sent you a copy, password protected."

"No, no, it's not safe!" Ann squeaked.

"I know. I sent it to you in the mail."

"E-mail?"

"No, I would never do that! I put it on a chip and mailed it to you, United States Post Office. I sent it to your home address."

"Ah, smart boy."

"No problem." Nicholas' fingers scurried around the keyboard for a few seconds and then stopped cold. "President Kinji?"

"I'm still here." Ann held her breath. Whatever he was about to say, she was sure she wasn't going to like it.

"I did a scan on the men. The system could ID them."

"And?"

"Is anyone with you?"

"Just my security detail."

"It's your security detail."

"Right. No one else, just my security detail."

"No. I'm saying, it's your security detail. On the footage. It's your guys."

12

"Sorry to interrupt your meeting, Miss Serena, but something happened." Nicholas stood behind Serena's head, speaking to her in a low tone.

Serena stood from her chair and addressed the Think Tank. "Excuse me."

Beav gave her a questioning look which she answered by jerking her head in the direction of the Think Tank. Beav nodded. "I'll take over if you can't make it back in? Five? Ten?" Serena

149

turned back in mid-stride and held up one hand, her fingers splayed. Beav called out, "Five minutes. We'll wait five minutes and then resume."

Serena pulled up a chair alongside Nicholas'. She looked at his screen. "President Ann's security detail. Why?"

"They dragged Lehman to use him to get past the iris scanner. They got into the records room."

"This is disturbing. You told the President?"

"Yes."

"Good. Anything else?"

"She's still with them, with the security detail."

"Oh no! Well, that's not good."

"What do we do?" Nicholas grimaced.

"We tell Estep."

"On it." Estep had been behind her the entire time. One step ahead of her, he had already alerted his team.

"Do you need me or Beav?" Serena stood up and called to his disappearing back, a method of communication that had become routine.

"I don't see the point of that." Estep was out

the door before she could reply.

Serena sank back into her chair with such force that the wheels shot backward and she almost took a dive. "Oh no, oh no, no, no."

Nicholas stared at her. "What?"

"The next in line to the President is the Vice President and Lehman is flat out on his back in the hospital. The next in line is the Speaker of the House, and he's... He's *here*."

Serena returned to the Think Tank. She didn't sit down. "There's a situation."

13

"Before we get dramatic, nothing has happened to the President," said Speaker of the House Joe Smythe.

"But shouldn't you be back at The Cube?" Serena had done it again. How her attempts to help always ended up convoluted and bungled, she didn't know. At least no one in the Think Tank had died, not yet anyway.

Joe looked at his phone and put it back in his pocket. "No. I should stay here. Unless I get a call, I'm better off participating in this history-making event you've set up. Let's do this."

Serena made eye contact with as many Think Tank members as possible. "Since we could be interrupted at any time, let's agree that everyone should get to the point quickly. When I move on to the next person, don't take it personally. We don't have the luxury of time. Let's start with Eric Dittelman. Why did you contact The Supporters?"

Dittelman pushed his glasses up his nose, being one of the few people left on the planet who still wore glasses. "I was invited to The Cube to entertain last week. It was for an appreciation day, for interns."

Beav interrupted. "An appreciation day during an national crisis?"

Dittelman continued, "President Kinji planned to meet with me but had to cancel. The Cube is a big place. Business as usual in one wing doesn't have anything to do with what happens in the President's wing."

"Go on," Serena encouraged. She frowned at Beav. "Let him finish his story, hold questions to the end."

Dittelman was visibly relieved to finally get his part over with. "Like I said before, President Kinji had to cancel her appearance at the preshow luncheon, but the First Gentleman attended. I noticed that he had a strange bruising around his right eye. I made a joke that President Kinji didn't like his politics. He said that he got the bruise from a faulty iris scanner. Later, I did my show and had a meet and greet photo op and signing afterward. I noticed that one of the interns had the same bruising on her right eye. It was a strange pattern, unmistakably the same as the First Gentleman's, and it couldn't have been random."

Dittelman said all of this at a hurried pace and then stopped. Serena waited for him to continue and when it was clear that he was finished she said, "I'm not sure I understand the situation."

Dittelman explained, "Interns don't have security clearance that requires the use of an iris scanner – at least not the one outside the Gallery. I forgot to add that little detail."

"Oh! I think I get it now. What was the intern doing in the high-security wing for top government only? She was not assigned to anyone there?"

Joe raised his hand.

Serena laughed. "You don't have to raise your hand, Mr. Speaker. Go ahead."

"I can answer this one. Dittelman is right. Interns most certainly do not have security clearance to be in that wing so even if she was somehow included in something going on up there, which I highly doubt, she wouldn't have been using the scanner herself. Someone else would have let her in with a guest pass, hand-verified by the security guards. There's absolutely no scenario in which an intern would have used that particular scanner."

Beav, his mind always racing straight to the technical, asked, "Are we sure that it's the only iris scanner that has had issues? Is it possible that the same malfunction, and therefore same bruising pattern, could be happening with other scanners in The Cube?"

Luke jumped in. "We verified that there was only one malfunctioning iris scanner. Our group investigated Dittelman's story right away. That's what we do."

"Nicholas, are you hearing all of this?" Serena called toward the front of the lab where Nicholas was still sitting at his computer. Serena worried about that boy's physical health.

Nicholas answered, "Yes, I'm looking into it now."

Luke tipped the bill of his cap over his face at the sound of Nicholas' voice. He really *is* paranoid, thought Serena. She had to strain to hear what Luke was saying.

"He'll be able to confirm what I said. Maintenance records for government buildings are public record if you know where to look."

"I believe you, but before we run off accusing people we'll double check everything we say here." Serena smiled diplomatically at Luke. She didn't know if she liked that kid or not; his overconfidence rubbed her the wrong way. Serena leaned across Beav to reach Dittelman. She patted him on his arm. "Eric, thank you for coming forward with this, and for meeting with us here in person."

Beav added, "I wish we had time for you to do one of your mind-reading routines for us."

Serena added her ditto and moved the session

along. "Mr. Speaker, please go next."

Joe stood up as if delivering a political speech. His full height was ordinarily on the taller side of average, but when he was standing while everyone else was seated, he towered over them like a beanpole giant. "I want to confess that I've been running my own private investigation. In part, I've been doing this to clear my own name, since it was obvious that I was on the list of suspects from day one. But also, I caught on quickly, shortly after I became Speaker, that I had stepped into something funky. People didn't look me in the eye, people stopped talking when I entered a room. Records went missing. People avoided answering my questions. I didn't want to come off as paranoid, so I kept my thoughts to myself and hired two separate private investigation firms that specialize in high-level cases. I got my money's worth, both were discreet and got the job done."

Luke raised his index finger. "Not as discreet as you might think."

Joe faced Luke. "What do you mean? What do you know about this?"

"One of your guys went straight to me,

straight to The Supporters anyway. In fact, he's the source of most of our information," said Luke.

Serena said, "You two can tag-team this story, fill in each other's gaps."

Both men looked at Serena dismissively before Joe resumed speaking. "The investigators didn't uncover much, but it was enough for me to have a good idea of what was going on. Senator William Casey and Senator Robert Lorry – the two senators that President Kinji called out – those two are definitely involved. Each of them has a mutiny in the works, recruiting more crew members every day. These ties can be traced back to the top, to Governor Carson, and beyond."

Joe stopped talking and sat back down.

Serena followed up with, "And you say you have evidence that connects these men?"

Joe replied, "It's all there in Carson's phone and Internet records. It should have been brought to your attention already."

Luke cleared his throat. "Actually, these records have been covered up. They never made it past the federal agencies who recovered them."

Joe's face registered genuine surprise. "Then how?"

Luke advised, "Mr. Speaker, you can neither confirm nor deny that you know anything about those records. Mahesh and Kobin can shed a little light on this."

There was a second or two of awkwardness as Mahesh and Kobin worked out who would speak. Kobin won the mental rock, paper, scissors. He quickly explained in layman's terms how they retrieved the information. "We hacked into the FBI. Or, rather, we hacked into one of their agents' server accounts."

Luke took back the reigns. "The records never made it past the FBI and other agencies involved. If you look into the evidence locker you won't find any of Governor Carson's electronics."

Joe stroked his chin. "The plot thickens. I must say that I find it rather disturbing that you were able to hack into classified FBI communications. I hope the end justifies the means—but I can't promise you that I won't look into this. Well, that's basically all I've got.

I thought I had something to offer but it sounds like this group was already onto it."

Luke said, "I wouldn't have told you anything if you could catch us. All you have is a story, which I will recant."

Jo spoke up for the first time since the meeting started. "Mr. Speaker..."

"Joe." His voice dropped into a lower register that was intimately masculine.

"Joe." Jo repeated. Her face flushed; her fair skin gave her away every time.

Serena and the rest of the Think Tank watched the flirting play out, all of them wondering if they should avert their eyes, but none of them willing to turn away. Serena prompted, trying to divert the runaway train back onto the right track, "Jo? You had something to add?"

Both Joe and Jo looked at her as if they had forgotten she was there.

Serena made a "heh" sound and clarified. "Joanna, do you have something to add?"

"I know that Luke can be a little hard to take, but in his defense, when a government buries information only extreme measures will uncover it. And yes, the end justifies the means. What I wanted to say though is that the reason why we looked into Governor Carson Landon's records is because we got a ping from Mr.—uh, Joe's—investigator. Joe, if you hadn't initiated an investigation, we wouldn't have gotten the tip."

"I'm relieved that I was able to contribute." Joe smiled.

Joe was about to say something more to Jo but Serena cut him off before the train could derail again. "Moving along to The Supporters. Luke, do you have anything more for us?"

Taking a cue from Joe, Luke stood up for his turn to speak, but when he heard Nicholas sneeze he abruptly sat down. "I have a filing cabinet full of evidence. We have traced communications, we have transcripts, we have documents. What's funny is that most of this is public record. They are hiding in plain sight."

Serena said, "If they are so blatant, why? Do they think they'll get their agenda in place before we catch up to them? Or are they so arrogant that they think we can't possibly catch on?"

Luke said, "Probably both. We have enough

to bury them, and enough to know that an assassination plot is in the works. We also have a few international names to add to the list of domestic traitors. What we don't know are the details of the plot."

Paul, who had been uncharacteristically silent since the moment he shuffled into the room, said, "I do."

14

Before Paul could say anything more, the Think Tank was shut down by the return of Agent Estep. Estep burst into the rectangle, taking center stage. His posture was that of a knight who had valiantly slayed a dragon. "President Kinji is safe. She is in an undisclosed location and will remain there for the time being. Mr. Speaker, please come with me."

There was an exit of controlled chaos as Estep and Joe hurried out of the lab. Quick-thinking Beav arranged for two members of Estep's team to escort Eric Dittelman home, with instructions to provide Dittelman 24 hour surveillance for his protection. Eavesdropping on that arrangement created panic in most of the Think Tank members as they realized for the first time that all of them were potentially in danger.

Serena gasped. "Nicholas!"

Nicholas responded. "Yes, I was able to verify everything said so far."

Serena held up her index finger to indicate that the group should wait for her. She walked over to where Nicholas was. "No, that's not what I meant. Nicholas, this has gotten out of hand. Once again, I've put your life in danger. It's time for me to call your parents."

"I've done things like this before," Nicholas protested. "Can I hear what Marco has to say first?"

Serena had forgotten about poor Marco. "I'll ask him to speak right away so that you can go immediately afterward. Better yet, I'll dismiss him too—neither one of you should be here."

Serena returned to the Think Tank with

Nicholas, who sat next to Beav in Dittelman's vacant seat. She addressed Marco. "I'm sorry you've been waiting all this time. You had raised your hand earlier, indicating that you have evidence to share."

Marco's left leg bobbed up and down in a tic-like fashion. He spoke in restricted prosody, a classic characteristic of someone diagnosed with Asperger's syndrome. "I was watching videos and the ones I wanted didn't stream. I had to get to the server myself to retrieve the ones I wanted."

Beav's ears perked up. "You hacked into the prison server?"

"No. I hacked into the Cloud."

Beav whistled in admiration. "How did you get past the prison firewall?"

"I'm not in an adult prison. The youth facility has a weak firewall. It was easy."

Serena noted that Marco seemed more relaxed now that he was talking about computers. "Marco, what did you find?"

Marco didn't make eye contact but he launched smoothly into the rest of his story. "I saw other videos. They didn't run right. Video files overlapped. I wanted to know why so I looked at the code. I saw another video file embedded in the one that was displayed. The overlap was hiding something else. I copied the code and..."

"Marco, you can tell Beav how you did it later, but for now, please tell us what you saw." Serena gently prodded.

"I saw them giving instructions."

"What kind of instructions?" Serena had a sinking feeling that she knew what he was going to say.

"Instructions on how to kill President Ann Kinji, and how they would get their money."

"Oh my. Thank you for telling us about this Marco. Did they discuss details about when this is supposed to happen or where?" Serena kept her voice calm despite the alarm bells ringing in her head.

"No. That's all I saw. Can I go home now?"

Serena felt tears stinging her eyes. She blinked them away and took a breath. "I'm sorry, Marco, I can't do that for you today. But I promise that we'll help you, even if I have to go to the President."

"If they don't kill her," said Marco simply.

"Yes, if they don't kill her." Serena knew that it wasn't the right time to wallow in this child's situation. She wrapped things up. "Thank you for being brave enough to share what you know. Now it's time for both you and Nicholas to go. You've both served your country well today. I'm proud of you."

Bob initiated a standing ovation. Every remaining member of the Think Tank stood up as the two boys- as well as Marco's prison guard escort, Nicholas' father, and three of Estep's agents on loan for Nicholas' family- headed toward the exit. The applause carried on until they were all out the door.

While the group was still distracted Serena used the time to sneak in a quick text message. "I love you" was instantly sent to her husband and to all three of her kids' accounts.

When she noticed that everyone had settled down Serena resumed leadership of the ever-shrinking Think Tank. "Let's come back to you now, Paul. What details were you talking about?"

Paul glanced around the room as if he were

evaluating their trustworthiness. He let a dramatic pause hang before he dropped his bombshell, relishing in the spotlight. "The assassination is set to go down in 48 hours and counting." He made a show of looking at his watch. "Make that 42 hours."

Beav said, "If you knew this, why didn't you contact us right away? Why are you just now telling us this?"

Paul replied, "I've been blocked for months now, cut off from the world. It doesn't matter, I knew you'd be in touch."

Serena shivered. While she had good naturedly taken her relationship with con-artist sociopath killer-of-two-presidents Paul in stride, over the past year he had developed a stalker-like fixation on her. Nonetheless, he was a valuable resource and she knew it. Unfortunately, so did he. In fact, Serena suspected that Paul worked tirelessly and obsessively to be an asset not out of patriotic duty but for the express purpose of gaining access to her.

Paul had nothing else to share but he was loath to admit it. He shot daggers at Victor when

Victor volunteered to speak next.

Serena hesitated, thrown off balance by the disturbing possessiveness Paul was displaying so Beav stepped in to keep things rolling along. "Go ahead, Victor."

Victor, who had earned his criminally insane title when he torched his old chemistry lab with his co-workers still inside it, was quite the specimen. He spoke now in such a personable and rational way that it was hard to imagine that he was capable of such a monstrosity. "We can still access the crack in the Social Media Channel. The prison system hasn't been upgraded. We can still see their messages."

"What did you see?" asked Beav.

"I didn't see anything, but Lita did." Victor pointed to Lita, even though Beav and Serena knew who she was, as they had been uncomfortably close to dying by her hand.

Lita tossed her long hair, hair that hadn't seen shears in months. She didn't care about split ends in prison. "It's nice to be a part of this. I hardly get a chance to talk to anyone in the outside world."

Serena grimaced. It was harder than she

thought it would be to interact with the criminally insane club. "Tell your story, Lita."

Lita cackled and said nothing.

Tristan spoke up. "Perhaps I can be of help."

Serena sighed. "Please."

Tristan grabbed one of the five chairs that were unoccupied and moved it directly in front of Lita. He positioned himself so that the two of them were face-to-face. "Lita, focus. What do you know?"

Lita looked into his eyes and began thrashing her head around. Her hair was a tangled blur. It was like watching the Tasmanian Devil in a Looney Toons cartoon.

Tristan placed both of his warm hands on Lita's knees. His hair fell over one of his eyes as he bent forward. With steady deliberation he placed his face precariously close to the whirling madness of head tossing and teeth gnashing. Lita's armed escort popped up beside them, ready to restrain her if necessary.

Lita responded to Tristan's touch by freezing in mid-motion. Her hair drifted slowly onto her back and shoulders. She blinked at him a few times before her face twisted into a seductive leer that went unnoticed by Tristan. He was too busy addressing his audience, "See now? She's like a wild animal in need of a little taming."

Beav crooked his finger in a frantic aerial point-point-point motion. "Uh, buddy, you might want to…"

It was too late. Lita kissed Tristan full on the lips and then head-butted him. The whole thing happened too fast for the guard to stop her. Tristan was knocked out cold.

"Oh no, I thought we'd make it through without any casualties," said Serena.

"You thought wrong," said a new voice they hadn't yet heard.

Serena, Beav, Luke and several others leapt to their feet. Three of the armed prison guard escorts also rose. There was momentary confusion when the group thought that the guards were standing to protect them. The guards' intentions became clear when they leveled their guns at Serena.

Serena Wilcox Bridges, the petite dark haired green-eyed private detective wife to Tom, mother to Carrie, Sam and Rebecca, personal friend and contract hire of the President of the

United States, was reflecting on the possibility that she would die today. As time stood still, something primal kicked in for Serena.

She was blinded by the vision of her children's faces. *You will not break the hearts of my babies!* Her battle cry was a scream not unlike the sound of a helium balloon that had been stretched to maximize a slow ear-splitting release. She charged forward with her weapon-less arms thrust out in front of her, the element of surprise her only real offense.

Shots rang out by the dozens. When the noise stopped, Serena surveyed the resulting carnage and said in an unnaturally bright tone, "Why this got a little more violent than anticipated. I'm glad I had the foresight to send the boys out."

The guards were laying on the floor, writhing around in agony. One of them managed to maintain his grip on his gun. Luke darted toward him and for a second the guard looked confused. The guard's eyes then re-focused and zeroed in on his target. He aimed the gun directly at the man on the other side of the room and fired.

Paul Tracy never saw it coming. His eyes had been on Serena. He had been rehearsing what new juicy information he would share when his heart felt strangely hot. Paul put his hand on his chest and slowly pulled it away—it was covered in his own blood. He knew he was going to die and he thought about his brother Clyde. *Was this what Clyde felt?* He looked at Serena, the woman he would never have. All the plans he had made for the future were fading along with his heart. He opened his mouth to speak but no words escaped.

15

President Ann Kinji was brought up to speed with what happened in what was already known as The Kneecap Massacre. As the miserable would-be assassins found out the hard way, one should never bring a gun into a meeting full of vigilantes. No fewer than six shooters (all from The Supporters) obliterated the kneecaps of the prison guards from the adult criminally insane facility, thus ending the first and last assembly of Serena's Think Tank with a fanfare. There was but one fatality, the guards' true target: Paul

Tracy. It seemed that Paul knew even more about the assassination than what he had already shared. Typical Paul, he was holding back to milk the attention. Now he would never have his final bask in Serena's spotlight.

"I don't want to be briefed in detail. This is your operation. Leave me out of it," said Ann.

Her private de-brief meeting with Agent Estep was held at her safe house. Estep had broken protocol, had jumped through hoops, and had taken a buzz saw to the red tape between himself and the president's undisclosed location. He refused to accept that he had done all of this only to be dismissed without being heard.

Agent Estep began his rebuttal. "I made the decision to read you in because this situation shortens our time window for flying under the radar. The prison guards were due back at the facility. We stalled off notice by putting our own people in their place. But someone will notice that the prison guards have been replaced by our people, and of course Paul Tracy didn't make it back. It's only a matter of time before the jig is up."

"You can't read the prison administration in?

I don't see why you are involving me." Ann reached for her sandwich, the first bite of food she'd had in over twenty-four hours.

Estep explained, "We suspect that the corruption at the prison goes higher than the prison guards. Someone will report this to whoever they work for, and we still don't know who that is. Reading them in will give them more information faster."

"I'm already in an undisclosed location, sitting on the sidelines of the presidency." Ann tossed her barely-touched sandwich on the table in front of her.

"This is going to get much worse. We've poked a stick in the hornet's nest. I think we should admit defeat on this one, Madam President." Agent Estep glowered at his feet. If his career wasn't already toast, surely it was dead now.

"Stop the cryptic gibberish and come out with it."

"You need to give up on the idea that your friends can play detective. Serena Wilcox investigating high-level government corruption? She almost died today. Her idea of defending herself was to scream like a banshee and run directly at her attackers."

Ann grabbed a pencil and chewed on the eraser. "She's a survivor."

"Even cats have only nine lives... Madam President, I strongly suggest that you pull her out."

"I hear you, but let me ask you this, did Serena's Think Tank end in a bloody mess?"

"You know that it did." Estep couldn't follow the president's train of thought in the slightest but he did see enough of the track ahead to know that wherever this was going he wasn't likely to have a job at the end of the tunnel.

"Then Operation Bluebird Flown is working. She's drawing them out of the sewers. She's like a Pied Piper to the rats. Stay on Serena – let her do what she does."

Estep felt uneasy, but why? He rolled President Kinji's words over and over in his mind until he was aware of why he felt a twinge on his conscience. "I don't feel comfortable using Serena as bait. She's a civilian."

Ann raised her eyebrows. When she

recovered from Estep's unexpected protest she said, "Exactly. Until we know more about who is committing treason and who isn't, we can't trust anybody in the government." Ann bit the entire eraser off the pencil and then spit the eraser into the trash.

Estep pretended not to notice. He was, however, too distracted by the eraser spew to formulate a thought.

Ann leaned across the table until her face was inches away from his. "How much power do you think I have as President?"

Stunned by the question, Estep was again at a loss for words.

"I'll answer that question for you: I'm powerless. My administration has been infiltrated, if it was ever mine in the first place. I've been blocked and bugged. I've been kept in the dark. I need information and Serena's the one to get it to me. Do you really think I'd use Serena as bait? I call upon her because she has an uncanny knack for finding the right people – she's a natural at bringing unlikely people together who somehow complete an overall human puzzle. When we were at the brink of apocalypse, only government insiders and powerful people had an inkling of what was to come, yet Serena just happened to have a friend who heard from a friend in Iraq. Serena got herself and her family to safety. She then managed to bumble about until she connected with none other than Paul Tracy. I don't understand how she attracts the right, or the so-wrong-they-are-right, people, but she does. What did she do with the Think Tank – who was there?"

Estep stared at her blankly. "I thought you didn't want details."

Ann sighed. "I need another pencil."

"President Kinji, I'm having a hard time keeping up with you."

"Ah, Estep. You're right, sorry for giving you whiplash. As much as I'd love to know what bizarre conglomeration of assorted oddball characters Serena assembled, I can't delve into this right now. I know that the Speaker of the House was included in that motley crew and I'm burning with curiosity on how that all went down. But you are right. I can't know the details. This is far from over. When the dust clears, there will still be an American government left standing in the rubble; and at the heart of the ruin will be the office of the President of the United States. The more bits and pieces I know, the more of this absurdity taints the office and I owe it to future administrations to leave the office a better place. When I'm a private citizen again I can call upon Serena for a cup of coffee and a long chat about who was involved in the Think Tank. I can satisfy my curiosity then. For now, you are right to remind me that I don't want details."

Estep gave up. "So you are insisting that Serena stay on."

"Let me tell you something. Serena wanted you specifically. Because of her, you're heading up the most important operation in possibly all of history. Think about that the next time you have the urge to tell me that Serena doesn't know what she's doing."

"Understood." Estep stared at his feet.

"While you're here, I want to give you a heads-up. I'm about ready to do something about that presidential impotence I was talking about. And when I do, I need your best profilers and snipers on hand. Consider this a hostage situation because it will be."

"Have you received threats? I mean beyond all of this? Has someone given you a direct threat?"

"No."

"I'm sorry, I can't for the life of me follow you and I've been trying." Estep scratched his head like a confused cartoon character might do.

"I'm the one making threats."

"Threats to?"

"Congress. But never mind that. Be there with your team in case they don't go away quietly."

Estep groaned. "I thought you'd call upon DHS to handle it."

"Is there a problem, Agent Estep?"

"No, no problem."

Ann stood up, slipped a piece of paper into Estep's hand, and opened the door for him to exit. "And Estep?"

"Yes?"

"With or without Serena. Your call."

"But you said…"

"Never mind what I said."

16

Serena's teenage son changed his favorite T-shirt, breaking a 72 hour wear-a-thon. Her daughters cleaned the guest bathroom. Serena and Tom cleared clutter and shut bedroom doors. The family ate a quick lunch of leftover taco meat on tortillas before the kids retreated into the family room downstairs. The trace of onions was still heavy in the air when Agent Estep rang the doorbell.

The first thing Estep noticed when he entered

the house was an upright piano topped with picture frames and candles. He wondered who played the piano. *Surely not Serena?* He couldn't imagine her having the patience to study music. As for himself, he had been forced to take piano lessons alongside his sisters. He was tempted to sit on the bench and tickle the ivories; he hadn't played in years.

"Would you like something to eat? A cookie?" Serena held out a plate of oatmeal chocolate chip cookies.

Estep laughed.

"I'll take that as a no." Serena started to pull the plate away but Estep's hand shot out, snagging two cookies.

"It's hard to take you seriously when you're in all-out mom mode, offering me cookies."

Estep took a large chewy bite.

Tom returned from his workshop in the garage and shook Estep's hand. "The president wants her back?"

The thought of leaving home again was already twisting Serena's stomach into knots. She had been under the impression that she was off the case.

"No, this time it's me," said Estep.

Serena and Tom exchanged a puzzled look. Serena said, "What do you mean, it's you?"

Estep sank into the couch without an invitation to sit. "I mean, she gave me the option to include you or not."

Tom said, "And you chose to include her?" His voice held an incredulous note.

"Against my better judgment maybe, but President Kinji is right. Serena has a way of bringing the right people together, people I'd never think could be useful. It's like she can read their minds." Estep looked wistfully at the kids' empty milk glasses on the side tables.

"You want milk with those cookies?" Serena asked.

Estep nodded.

"It was easy to get inside your head just now, Estep. Deep down we all want a Mom. Even Moms want a Mom. Get inside people's heads and you'll be able to guess what motivates them, what drives them, and what makes them want to kill." Serena said all of this while pouring a glass of milk in the kitchen, her voice barely heard from where Estep was sitting in the living room.

Estep groaned. "I could respect you easier if you wouldn't talk so much."

Tom walked into the kitchen, took the glass of milk from Serena's hand and said, "I've got this." Even though Estep was a tall and broad shouldered young man in his twenties, he suddenly seemed like a sullen teenager in his low-seated position on the family couch.

Serena returned to the room. Both she and Tom remained standing. They watched Estep drink his milk. "The mission is dangerous," he said.

Tom grabbed Serena's arm. "You don't have to do this."

Serena nodded. "I know." She folded her arms across her chest. She asked Estep, "Why do you need me?"

"I want you to do whatever it is that you do to make all the crazy happen. My plan is to do exactly as I'm trained to do. I'll get the snipers in place, I'll put the profilers in the room, I'll bug the place, I'll do it all by the book. What you do is…"

"Magical?" Serena offered.

Estep sighed noisily, dramatically. "I don't know what you do. Can you just do it? This has to happen tonight."

Serena looked at Tom. Tom said, "Take me with you."

"No-can-do sir. Not a good idea." Estep rose from the couch and handed Serena his drained milk glass.

Serena took the glass from him without saying a word. Her heart was in her throat– while she had been watching bad guys get their knees blown to bits she had missed her youngest daughter's last visit from the Tooth Fairy. She put Estep's empty milk glass in the kitchen and viewed the clutter of the room.

This was *her* kitchen, but she hadn't spent any real time in it for so long that the room didn't feel like her space anymore. Used freezer bags on the counter tops told the story of how her family had been living off of the casseroles she had baked ahead for them. The pile-up of pizza boxes told the tale of what her family did when they were weary of eating frozen casseroles. Dinner with her family was one of her favorite times of the day and she had given that up for over two months. As she felt a tear slide down her cheek she promised herself that this would be her last operation.

The kitchen seemed to wave goodbye to her. Its cheerful lighting, its red and yellow décor, its cooktop stove with its baked-on mess, and its new additions of a lingering smell of onions and a platter littered with cookie crumbs all cried out for her to stay.

But staying wasn't an option when she was so certain that she should see this through. She really did have a gift and she believed she had a moral obligation to use that gift, especially when lives depended on it. She told herself that she could catch up on family time when the job was done.

Once in the car she had second thoughts. She prayed silently for validation that she was doing the right thing. Estep respected her time of reflection simply because he was relieved that Serena wasn't talking. Serena looked out the passenger side window and felt her spirit sinking further and further as each familiar milestone slid out of view. Then she did a double-take. She saw a moving billboard that alternated between two randomly selected ads. One was a recruitment slogan for a local university. It said, "The world needs people like you." The other was an advertisement for a real estate agency. The image depicted a happy family, two parents and three kids, in a kitchen with yellow and red décor. The slogan read, "Because at the end of the day, they're waiting for you at home."

Serena giggled.

Estep glanced at her. "What's so funny?"

"God works in mysterious ways. I asked for a sign and I literally got not just one sign but two. And by literally I mean that these are actual signs."

Estep raised an eyebrow. "Am I supposed to ask what this is all about?"

Serena noticed a look of annoyance creeping into Estep's expression. She sighed. "No, I'm good. Tell me about the mission. Is this still a part of Operation Bluebird Flown?"

"Yes, it was never closed. It's all a mess though. I'm not sure Covert Coffee ever ended. It doesn't matter what we call it."

Serena, having been given her sign, was ready to give her 110%, which she expressed by jumping back into the game with both feet. "Fill me in."

"President Kinji is getting UN backing to temporarily gain full authority over the nation, superseding Congress."

"Oh my, she got what she wanted! That's a drastic measure for sure. She'll make a lot of new enemies."

"And will provoke the enemies she already has."

"You're needed for security then, and in anticipation of investigating whatever happens, you'll be proactive in recording the event, surveillance, and the usual."

"Correct."

"What you need from me is a covert team that the official covert team doesn't know anything about, in other words, my usual."

"Yes."

"First you have to get Beav. We need him on the B team. B stands for Badass by the way."

Estep's voice was flat. "No."

"But Beav is our best guy."

"I mean, no, don't ever say 'badass'."

"You're getting Beav?"

"Yes."

"Good. I also want The Supporters."

"So far you've been highly predictable. Maybe I didn't need you after all."

"Oh really? Well I bet you'll be surprised by my last three picks."

"Speaker of the House?"

"Why would I want him?" Serena scoffed.

"Why did you want him last time?"

"I was trying to rule him in or out as a suspect. I had a gut feeling he was one of the good guys but I had to be sure. He's solid. I wouldn't want to put him in harm's way or bring down his reputation by attaching this operation to him any more than we already have."

"The nutters from the criminally insane netherworld?"

"No, no. We got what we wanted from them, which wasn't much this time."

"All right, I give up. Who?"

17

Serena waited for Beav to get in the car before revealing who else she wanted on her team. Beav had been waiting for them outside a movie theater where he had been working concessions. Why he was working there, they didn't know. They had learned that with Beav there was never a simple explanation; unless there was time for storytelling, it was best not to inquire.

"I want the intern," said Serena. "The one

that Eric Dittelman told us about, with the iris scanner bruising on her face."

"Ah-hah!" Beav clapped his hands together. "I've been working on that."

Estep admitted, "I'd forgotten all about her."

"What did you learn?" asked Serena.

Beav grinned. He had worked a shift at the theater after a grueling workout. He was now in overdrive. "I bet you are wondering why I was at that particular cinematic location?"

"Not particularly," said Estep.

"She works there," Beav gloated.

"Then why are we still driving away from the theater? Let's go back and get her!" Serena said.

"No, we don't need her," said Beav. "I got all the relevant intel, easy-peasey. Sharing a ride with her would be annoying, trust me."

"Fill us in," said Serena.

"Typical story—she was having an affair with a politician. He asked her to retrieve something from the room, a bug. She did it, end of her involvement."

"You're sure of that?" asked Estep.

"Oh yeah, I'm sure. I went to great lengths to vet her. The things I had to do…" Beav grimaced.

"Oh no, you didn't?" Serena gulped.

Beav threw his head back and laughed. "No, of course not! I had to listen to her gum-smacking jaw-jabbering barely coherent confessional. Excruciating! Women shouldn't enter this world until they're at least 30."

Serena wasn't sure whether to agree or disagree. "That's an odd tangent, even for you. Moving along, what did she say?"

"That was it. I've skipped all the pointless minutia. Her boyfriend dumped her after she was done spying for him. I had to hear all about that. She did mention that she got access to the iris scanner through temporary top security clearance. Sometimes a temporary clearance is granted for the purpose of entering an area for a final interview process before an inner-departmental hire. Because she was already working at The Cube, her information was already on file. Someone only needed to upload it into the iris scanning software for that reader. So, what we're looking for is a person who had access to the scanning software. The official team at The Cube can handle that small detail."

"Aren't you going to tell us who the politician boyfriend is?" asked Serena.

"Silly me, that's the fun part. Senator Robert Lorry." Beav flashed a triumphant smile.

"Lorry, I knew it. One of the prime suspects is confirmed," said Estep.

"I'm glad I could do that, but President Kinji wanted us to look beyond the obvious. I was disappointed when she said his name. I was hoping for a new lead," said Beav.

Estep said, "Nice job though. It means we don't have to pick her up, whoever she is. You didn't even tell us her name."

Serena spoke up. "I think I know her name."

Beav said, "Really? Go for it."

"Breyana."

Beav yelped. "What? How did you get that?"

"Breyana is President Kinji's assistant. When you were talking about the boyfriend motive for spying I thought of all the young female interns that would have had the best access to Ann's office in the past year. Breyana isn't an intern, but she looks young enough to be mistaken for one. She genuinely admires Ann, which is why we never considered her as a suspect. We were short-sighted; some girls will betray their best friends for love, and Breyana has the most access to Ann's office, and to Ann herself. I put two and two together."

"I wish I'd remembered that Breyana was President Kinji's assistant. I vaguely recall having seen her before now that I think about it, but she must have been quiet when I saw her. Believe me, if she had opened her mouth I would have remembered that voice. Still, I'm mad at myself for screwing this up!" Beav pounded his fist into his hand.

Serena laughed. "I never noticed anything wrong with her voice."

Beav grumbled, "You would have if you'd had to listen to her until your ears bled."

Estep started to turn the sedan around. "We're going back for her then?"

"No, keep going. Phone it in and let law enforcement pick her up. They can take it from here," said Serena.

Estep straightened the wheel. "Are you sure? I thought you wanted her on your team."

"Not anymore. She was used to spy on Ann and that's probably the extent of what she knows. Senator Lorry dumped her which means she's nothing to the inner circle. She's not worth our time."

Estep said, "Then tell me where I'm going."

"I was getting to that. Do you remember that President Kinji had someone with her when she called Nicholas, that day at the lab when we were there? Her name is Dr. Kendra Wellington."

Beav jumped in. "I remember. What do you think she can do for us?"

Serena pondered that for a moment. "I don't know, maybe nothing."

Estep scoffed. "Then why include her?"

Serena explained, "Because Ann trusts her."

Estep was impressed. "That actually makes sense. Who else?"

"One of the prison guards who had his knees blown off."

"What? No, I don't want somebody getting blood and pus all over the seats." Estep drummed his fingers on the steering wheel. "What do you want him for anyway?"

"Only one of them lawyered up right away. That's the one I want," said Serena.

Beav asked, "What's your thinking on that?"

Serena answered, "He's the one who's in contact with the bigger fish. He'll want a deal and I think we can get more out of him outside of an official investigation."

"He's still in the hospital, I assume?" asked Estep.

"He's about to be released," said Serena.

"When will this happen?" asked Estep.

Serena said, "When we release him of course! I think it's worth it to get him. Call it a hunch."

"Everything's a hunch with you," said Estep.

"He's as cheery as ever I see," said Beav.

"He chose me for this mission. His bite has no venom, " said Serena.

"Still, Estep, dude, you need to lighten up. I bet you have high blood pressure already. What are you, twenty-five or something? You need to find a new girl, or get yourself a good loyal dog," said Beav.

"Yes, that's what he needs—a dog!" Serena clasped her hands together, her eyes sparkling with the joy of her plans.

Estep snapped. "I'm not getting a dog!"

Serena turned around in her seat to face Beav. She whispered, "We're getting him a dog."

18

Ann's meeting was to be held deeply underground, in a large open space inside a cave – a hole so deep that spy satellites couldn't see it. Ann's people were the only ones who could record the event, thus protecting the misuse and doctoring of footage. And, although it was not her plan to do so, Ann herself needed to cover up a few truths should anything go wrong.

Veiled Abyss cave, discovered only within the past decade, was a popular tourist attraction.

However, as of four hours ago, it was eerily empty. All of the attraction's employees had been sent home, the entire area had been cleared out, and all of the inroads had been blocked off. A special ops team had swept the area and had set up shop in the largest space of the cave, an open area about a quarter of a mile from the cave entrance.

The gift store was located in the open area, which also served as a lobby where patrons could wait for their turn in the cave tour queue. President Kinji's set-up crew had removed all of the gift store's vendor equipment, product inventory, and everything else that wasn't nailed down. In its place they installed conference seating, two hundred chairs wedged in tightly.

Leg space was nearly non-existent, but comfort wasn't Ann's concern. Two hundred carefully selected guests would soon face the designated back cave wall, where a small podium had been erected and two rows of additional chairs on each side of the podium had been reserved. Counting herself, and all of her team who would remain standing, Ann was expecting two hundred and forty-nine people to gather inside Veiled Abyss, concealed and sheltered in what could well become a mass coffin.

Ann heard a noise and jumped. "Oh it's you!"

"I'm here. I have my inhaler with me, so I should be good." Serena took a deep breath that she instantly regretted. There was a funky odor in the cave that she couldn't quite place. *Bat guano? Mold? Snails? Do snails have a smell?* Serena studied the space, her eyes wide with claustrophobic terror.

"I see you've assembled another Serena special team," said Ann. She gestured to the three people who had separated themselves from the others. "I recognize the prison guard, the crutches gave him away. You'll have to explain to me later why you brought him here. And of course I know Kendra. I intended to invite her here myself. She had volunteered to attend significant events as a historical witness. How did you know about that? Or did you invite her here for some other reason? Well, you can fill me in later. She's a good choice. The only one I don't know is him – why did you bring a child with you?"

"He's Marco, a friend of Nicholas. He is profoundly gifted and has been unfairly imprisoned under the Proactive Imprisonment Act that allows the government to place youth at high risk for mass violence events into corrective mental facilities."

"Oh dear. You know that I opposed the Proactive Imprisonment Act. Just another example of how I have absolutely no real power in this country. But why did you bring Marco here? I can't guarantee his safety."

"It can't be any worse than what he's going through in the youth facility. He has an amazing gift of heightened perception. He's possibly our best asset."

"I'll allow it – but give me your digi pen."

Serena handed it over.

"I uploaded my signature seal. Marco is to be released immediately from his so-called corrective mental health facility. As soon as you are done with his involvement here, send him home."

Serena's face lit up. "Absolutely!"

"I have a few opening statements to make.

Afterwards, you'll have time to prep your team. Good luck to you and your people. Thank you for your service."

"Ann, let yourself be a real person for a minute. You need a hug." Serena rushed at her with open arms before Ann had a chance to respond. She gave Ann a quick squeeze and said, "I'll pray for you."

"Appreciated." Ann's eyes misted over. She abruptly turned away from Serena before her emotions got the better of her.

Five minutes later Ann was fully engaged in the task at hand, with her brief lapse into humanity already behind her. After all, lest she forget, she was President Ann Kinji; the first female President, the first Japanese-American President, and the first President ever to take control of Congress.

President Ann took the podium. "Please be seated."

Serena and her team obediently sat in the first row. "I thought you didn't want the Speaker in on this?" Beav whispered across Estep to Serena.

Serena said, "I didn't. Ann must have asked

Joe to come."

All heads had turned when Joseph Smythe entered the meeting space, but only one of them had Joe's attention in return. Joe maneuvered his way through the aisle, his lanky frame unable to handle the narrow space. He made a jumble of the chair alignment as he quipped "Sorry" and "Excuse me" while tripping over himself and everyone else on his way to the center of the room. After the noise from clanging chairs and clomping feet finally ceased Joe had settled upon a chair next to Jo, the curly-haired Supporter from Ireland.

However, that chair was already occupied by Bob, the affable radio show personality Beav first met after his late-night run from the cornfield in Indiana. Bob gave up his seat and moved to another chair further down the row. Joe embarked into the chair beside Jo in the most ungainly way imaginable.

Ann chastised, "Mr. Speaker, none of the other one hundred or so empty chairs appealed to you?" As she anticipated, a soft collective chuckle went up, and so did the red pigment on Jo's face.

She waited for complete silence before resuming. "I asked the Speaker of the House to come here today because I have confided in him my plans. He is completely on board with helping us with this mission."

She detected the collective exasperation rising from the peanut gallery. "I know, you have no idea what the mission is. I'm getting to that. First off, I want to express to each of you how grateful and appreciative I am that you are here today. The next few hours may be dangerous. If anyone has second thoughts, it is not too late to change your mind. However, you must leave now. Once I brief you, you cannot leave until the mission has ended." She amended her statement. "With the exception of young Marco, who will be escorted out when his role is completed."

Ann surveyed their faces and saw not a trace of regret on any of them. What she did see was curiosity and impatience, in all but Joe and Jo. The two of them were swooning over each other in their confined space in the dank and chill of the Veiled Abyss cave, moments before a briefing about the biggest covert operation of their lives, lives that were threatened to be cut short. Ann could think of worse first dates.

She moved on. "This mission is part of Operation Bluebird Flown, which originated as an operation to find and protect Serena Wilcox. While that situation was quickly resolved, Serena's involvement in helping me peel back the layers of government conspiracy has been ongoing. Therefore, Operation Bluebird Flown was never closed, but instead has evolved into today's events involving all of you."

She paused for a sip of water. "Serena has an uncanny knack for bringing the right people together, people who would normally never speak to each other, let alone work cooperatively on a joint venture. I trusted her to bring the right people here and I believe that she did. What I'm asking you, Serena's Dream Team is this: solve the investigation on the spot, live, while I'm speaking."

She noticed puzzled expressions on several of their faces. She attempted to explain. "As in, imagine me up here as I am now. Except, imagine that this is the real deal and I'm addressing my hand-selected people of interest, delivering the most important speech I will ever deliver. Before I reach the end of my speech, I want to see your hands in the air. I will call you up to the podium and you will reveal what you know. I want all the secrets out in the open before anyone leaves this place tonight."

Serena raised her hand.

"Yes?"

Serena got up from her chair and walked directly to the podium. "Just like this? Is this what you want us to do?"

"Yes. Come up here when you know who the remaining suspects are and tell me before it's too late. Your job is to watch what happens. Keep an eye on everyone and everything. I know that I'm asking a lot of you. You don't have your computers or the luxury of time. I'm asking for you to rely on your intuition and powers of observation. We can flesh out all the evidence later. What I want to know is who we need to detain for further questioning. I don't want any of the rats to slink out of here. If any of the guilty parties are let loose, her or she will head straight to the airport and there won't be any way to stop them. Because after I make my announcement, the culpable will know that the game is over. If you let them out the door, they're gone."

Serena asked what several of the others were wondering. "Why come to you at the podium? Why not tell Agent Estep and let his security detail take care of it?"

"I want all of you to see all the developments as they unfold, live. Think of it as mystery theater and you're the leading actors." Ann smiled. "I know that this is unorthodox, but I've learned from Serena to think outside of the box. I'm confident that this method of putting everything out on the table will generate the results I'm anticipating. By surrounding ourselves with solid witnesses to protect the integrity of how this event will be reported, portrayed, recorded, and presented in court we will even up the David verses Goliath odds. It's going to take all of us working together to fire the sling that will bring down this giant."

"We can do this," Serena assured her. When she looked out at the front row, she saw that Estep was aghast but everyone else looked agreeable.

Ann applied her wrapping-things-up tone of voice. "I want everyone in the room to know how fast we are circling the wagons. I also want our investigation to be out in the open where my journalist guests can see it for themselves. Everything must be recorded and everything must be above-board. When all the pieces come together live, for all to actively experience, we will have enough witnesses to validate what happens here tonight. While false accounts and conspiracy theories will develop despite our best efforts, we will have ample documentation to convince reasonable citizens that our version of the truth *is* the truth."

"And when will this happen?" Luke asked.

Ann waved him off. "Serena will conduct a briefing now. I'll turn it over to her. Before I do, I want to wish all of you a safe journey through this dangerous expedition. God have mercy on us all."

19

President Kinji left them to their own devices, presumably to collect her thoughts before the big event. Behind the counter in the cave's tourist information bay was a small office. Ann slipped into that office, alone, and shut the door. How she prepared herself was a mystery, but whatever it was, it always worked.

Serena clasped her hands together. "I have some ideas."

Estep put his head in his hands. Because he

was a large guy in the front row, it was a distraction that Serena had to ignore. Fortunately she had had plenty of practice with ignoring Estep's drama. "I know that this is a lot to take in and you probably feel like this will never work, but with some planning we can do this brilliantly."

Serena felt silly standing behind the podium. Standing at not-quite five two, all that could be seen above the podium was her face and neck. She imagined herself as a talking floating head. "Let's make a circle."

Estep muttered, "Again with the circle." Yet all of them, including Estep, popped up at once to comply. The din of clanking and clattering chairs echoed in the cave for what felt like an interminable period of time.

Once seated in a circle, they could now see each other's faces, which was the purpose of the exercise. Serena began. "We don't have much time so I'll dig right in. Marco, I have some happy news for you. When you are done working with us today, you can go home to your mom and dad. President Kinji has ordered that you be released. You're going home today,

Marco!"

Marco's expression didn't change much. "The cat will be there."

"Yes, the cat too. I'm glad you are going home, Marco. May I ask for your help now?"

"My mother says that I have a gift for focusing."

"Yes, you do. Marco, Paul Tracy was killed during the Think Tank session after you left. He knew information that powerful people do not want us to know about. I think you know what that information is."

"I do know what that information is."

"Will you please share that with us, Marco?" Serena held her breath, hoping that whatever he said next would be the break in the case they needed.

Marco spoke slowly and deliberately, at a volume that was difficult to hear. Everyone in the circle leaned forward. "Paul Tracy knew about RDAD. The assassination of President Ann Marie Kinji will occur in 1.32 hours."

Several in the group gasped. Serena whirled around at the offenders and held a finger to her lips. "Go on, Marco. Take your time. Please tell me what RDAD is."

"Re-Direct And Distract. It is an acronym."

When Marco didn't say anything more, Serena prompted him. "What does the acronym mean?"

"RDAD was developed in 1993. It is a strategy to redirect and distract the American people from the business of the government. The populace focuses on the decoy issue. The government focuses on the actual issue. I play chess. Do you play chess?"

Serena assumed that the correct response Marco was going for was yes. "Yes," she lied.

"The populace are pawns."

"I understand." Serena was relieved that his chess analogy was so basic. "Is there anything else you can tell me about RDAD?"

Marco didn't respond. He already looked fatigued. Serena moved on. "How does RDAD relate to President Kinji?"

"President Ann Marie Kinji is a pawn too."

Serena worked hard to grasp what he was saying. "But if she is a pawn, isn't she doing what the government wants? Why do they want her taken out?"

Marco's energy was renewed now that he was engaged in educating Serena about chess. His voice remained flat and unhurried, but he was much more talkative. "A pawn that advances all the way to the other side of the chessboard is typically queened, the pawn is promoted and has more power to win the game. President Ann Marie Kinji has been in office long enough that she will soon reach the end of the board. She will be queened."

Serena blinked her eyes slowly. "I'm trying to understand. Can you please explain your chess analogy to me?"

Marco looked down at his hands.

"Let me help," said Mahesh, one of the members of The Supporters.

Serena gestured for him to go for it.

Mahesh brought his chair close to Marco, until he was face to face with him; a move that made several of the former Think Tank members squirm and cringe, remembering how unfortunate the result was when Tristan did that to Lita. They breathed a sigh of relief when nothing happened.

Mahesh said, "Marco, I want to suggest

something to you. Please tell me if I am correct or incorrect. When you refer to President Kinji as being queened, you are saying that she will have the same abilities as more powerful chessmen, correct?"

"You are correct," Marco confirmed.

"President Kinji will soon learn about RDAD and she will not go along with it, am I correct?"

"You are correct." Marco confirmed.

Mahesh continued slowly, careful not to shut Marco down. "Because she will not go along with it, the people who use RDAD will be forced to stop using it, correct?"

"You are correct," he said again.

Mahesh kept going. "Because they don't want to stop using RDAD, they want President Kinji out of office. Correct?"

"You are correct."

Mahesh nodded. "Thank you, Marco. Ms. Wilcox may have some additional questions for you. If it's okay with you, I'd like to stay here next to you."

Marco said, "It is."

Serena mouthed "thank you" to Mahesh. "Marco, how will President Kinji learn about

RDAD?"

Marco looked tired again. "The United States has allies. The allies will tell her about RDAD at the next meeting of the Global Initiative."

Serena followed up, "Did you learn about this from hacking into the security crack in the Social Media Channel?"

"Yes, I did. Members of the Global Initiative had secret meetings in the security hole on the Social Media Channel. I could see them talking."

Serena hoped that Marco had enough juice left in him to address the most important matter. "Marco, please tell me everything you know about the plan to assassinate President Kinji."

"They want the assassination to happen before the next summit. Economic issues and world issues will be undermined if an American president interferes with the Global Initiative agenda." Marco stopped talking and looked meaningfully toward the cave tunnel.

"Wow, that's a lot of information, Marco! Thank you for sharing all of that. I'll let you go home to your parents soon. Please hold on for just a couple more minutes. Can you tell us anything that could help us stop the assassination from happening?"

"Yes." Marco stared straight ahead and said nothing more.

Serena prodded. "Please tell us."

"Men were hired to kill her but she is here in this cave. They won't find her when they wait for her outside of the scheduled press conference today. They will move to Plan B. They will kill her in here, in 1.13 hours."

Serena held her voice steady, speaking to Marco as calmly as if she were reading him a story. "What is Plan B, Marco?"

Marco pointed past Mahesh to the man directly across from him.

Chairs suddenly crashed to the cave floor, creating confusion, and a cloud of dust. People moved in all different directions while a few remained frozen in their seats. Someone, who later was identified as Beav, shouted, "The President!"

Ann heard the commotion coming from outside the tourist bay. She knew better than to poke her head out there. Her team would be safer if she didn't make herself more vulnerable by presenting herself as an easy target. She crawled under the only large piece of furniture in the room, a short metal desk.

She waited for what felt like an immeasurable period of time. Her life flashed before her, as she'd always heard can happen to those who recognize that this may be the end. She saw herself as a child, growing up in Warsaw, Indiana, about three hours' drive from The Cube in Chicago. She saw herself during happier times with her parents. She saw highlights of her entire married life with Ted through images that burst through her mind in a rapid-fire slideshow.

Funny how she didn't see her many accomplishments, not even the day that she was sworn in as President. No, all she saw were the people she loved, and the people who loved her.

She heard the sound of something hitting the wall separating the tourist bay office from the rest of the cave reception area. She heard two more thuds against the wall before the fourth airborne object burst through. She heard a hissing sound and then smelled something funky that she couldn't identify. She felt herself drifting away, looking over her prone body, curled up in a fetal position. As she hovered there, in that twilight between life and death, she mourned for the children she would never have.

20

The door flew open, slamming into the adjoining wall with such force that the plaster shattered as agents Meril and Banert from Agent Estep's team barreled into the office. Banert pulled Ann out from under the desk. "Come this way, Madam President."

He stopped short. "She's not breathing!"

Meril cried out, "What do we do?"

Estep appeared out of nowhere, barking,

"Pull it together! Do what you're trained to do!"

Banert and Meril stared at him, unable to move.

"Get out of the way!" Estep gently lifted the president in his arms and carried her into the open cave reception area. Beav ran to meet him, the on-hand emergency medical staff at his heels.

Beav spoke rapidly, but enunciated every word he said so that nothing would be misunderstood. "This is Cajan Powder. I know what this is, trust me. Do as I say. She has angioedema. You have to open her airway. Now."

No one questioned Beav's authority, but the approach to open her airway required a fast judgment call by an experienced surgeon. The most senior staff medic ruled out intubation, going straight to the last resort: a cricothyrotomy. He skillfully made a vertical incision on the skin of the neck of the President of the United States of America, something he would talk about for the rest of his life. He then stepped aside to give room for two of his medics to insert a tracheostomy tube and supply the president with a bag-valve device to administer oxygen.

"She'll be okay?" Serena asked the medic who had performed the emergency procedure.

"She needs to be hospitalized immediately, but she'll pull through, barring any complications."

Serena got out of the way and let the medical team pass. She and dozens of others parted into two lines of solemn observers as President Ann Kinji, her body small and still, was carried out on a stretcher. It was the first time any of them had seen her as anything but a tigress. Her fragility shocked them into collective silence; the only sounds were the clicking of swaying medical equipment, the steady dripping inside the cave, and the footsteps of the medics as they shuffled their way into the cave tunnel.

Even when medics were long gone no one moved. No one spoke. No one wanted to be the one who broke the silence. And yet, someone had to do it. Speaker of the House, Mr. Joseph Smythe, in his first opportunity to lead when it really mattered, stepped up.

He said, "We have to get back on task.

President Kinji will survive this and when she comes to, I want to tell her that we did our jobs. Let's get these demons and throw them back into the pit where they belong."

Serena signaled for everyone to return to the circle of chairs that now had four missing seats. She took a deep breath and again regretted it. The dank of the cave was getting to her. She focused her thoughts: *I need to shake off this feeling of Think Tank déjà vu. I can do this, I'm good under pressure.*

She began, "Let's begin with a debrief about what happened. President Kinji benefited from immediate medical care. Her top medical team used a surgical airway kit- not a straw, a ball point pen, or anything like that. She'll have an uneventful recovery and she will be released from the hospital in six days, if they can keep her there. She'll want to leave the hospital as soon as she is able to move."

Beav took over. "Allow me to cover the next issue, involving what occurred. The timeline we've established indicates that the device was assembled on site right under our noses. They carried the pieces in separately, sat next to each other, handed the pieces over to an assembler who then put the device together. This manner of smuggling parts of a weapon to assemble on site is typical; what's atypical is the brazenness and the arrogance of those involved. They did all of this while we were sitting together in the front row, while the President of the United States was speaking just a few feet away from them. They caught a few breaks that made this an easy task. For example, when we were distracted by Mr. Speaker tripping all over himself to sit next to Miss Irish Red- sorry, I'm blanking on your name- they would have had the cover they needed to assemble the noisier or more tedious parts of the weapon."

Both Joe and Jo blushed.

Beav carried on. "So the answer to 'how did they get that in here' is that they did it in pieces, none of which triggered an alarm when scanned separately. But I haven't figured out how they got the powder in. The powder would have had to have been encased in plastic. Agent Estep assures us that all of you were patted down thoroughly before entering the cave. How did we miss the Cajan Powder itself?"

Marco raised his hand.

Serena grimaced. She had forgotten that the child had witnessed the entire event. She pointed to him.

He said, "He didn't search everyone."

Agent Estep shook his head. "I assure you that everyone was searched."

Marco disagreed. "You didn't search her." He looked at Serena Wilcox Bridges, mother of three, the last person anyone would suspect of smuggling poison to kill the president, who had also become her dear personal friend.

Beav stood up, his chair falling backwards from the abrupt motion. He lunged toward Serena, who defensively shielded her face with her hands. He snatched her purse from her lap. "Your inhaler!"

He rummaged through her purse until he found the plastic instrument used to administer Serena's asthma medication. The plastic casing had no prescription label on it. "They switched it out before you went into the cave. That's how they got it in."

Serena's eyes were wild and big with terror. "You mean that I'm in a cave with no inhaler?"

Estep snapped, "The medics have oxygen, you're fine."

Beav accentuated the positive. "At least you didn't try to use it when it was still full of toxin. When did you leave your purse unattended?"

Serena retraced her steps in her memory. Recognition washed over her face. "I left it in the car when we were standing around waiting to get in. They could have gotten it then."

Beav nodded. "Definitely. It wouldn't have taken them more than a few seconds to switch out the inhalers. I wouldn't use that one by the way."

Estep snorted.

Serena ignored the pair of them. "I'm horrified that I brought the toxin in here, but I can't let my emotions slow us down. Moving on to the next question: Luke, how is it that no one in your group suspected your own members of being spies? I don't understand how they got past such a naturally paranoid group of people. Isn't your whole mojo about being suspicious of anyone and everyone?"

Luke said, "Obviously."

"What's done is done," Joe said. "What we

need to do now is move on quickly from this and prepare for the meeting. Ms. Wilcox will to have to fill in for President Kinji."

Beav leaned over and said in a low voice, "Can you do that?"

Serena assured him. "She left her notes on the podium. I know Ann—what she calls 'notes' is essentially an entire speech, word for word."

Bob voiced the concern that was on all of their minds. "When you're doing that, what are we supposed to do?"

Joe said, "Do what we originally planned. Come up to the podium when you discover anything suspicious."

Estep scoffed. "The odds of that far-fetched plan working were slim to none in the first place. We need to shut this thing down."

Beav's eyes narrowed. He stood up, so although he was the smaller man of the two, he seemed at that moment like the larger. "We'll carry out her plan, that's what she would have wanted us to do."

Estep stood. He dwarfed Beav. "She'd want us to do what needs to be done. We have to get everyone out of here."

Joseph Smythe stood. He dwarfed both of them. "Sit down."

All three men sat.

Serena said, "Thank you, Joe. We need to hurry to get this back on track before we run out of time. Here's what I want you to do: infiltrate into the crowd. The people in your immediate vicinity are your responsibility. I don't know what President Kinji's speech is, and I don't have time to look it over before we begin. I'm guessing that she wrote a few shock and awe points to deliberately provoke people into expressing guilt through their reaction to whatever bombshells she planned to drop. Remember, the guest list was chosen based on other suspicious behavior, so your observations are only one of the criteria that will earn them a seat on the detainment bus. Don't be afraid to point fingers based on little more than a hunch: President Kinji is counting on us to help her round these people up. Pay attention!"

Marco raised his hand.

By now everyone knew to listen to this kid when he spoke. All were straining to hear what he had to say. "I know what she wants."

Serena encouraged him to continue.

"She wants to know which members of the Global Initiative are traitors. Those are the people she can't track with our resources."

Serena agreed. "Yes, but since she didn't specify that, I think she wants us to watch literally every single person in the room. There may be surprises, like the one we just had. We vetted all the Supporters. I don't know what happened."

Luke offered up his theory. "Craig's wife has cancer and the medical bills were piling up. He could have been bought after he was cleared. Everyone has a price."

Serena waved them off, already mimicking something President Kinji would have done had she been there. "I'm not blaming you. We missed it too. I'm merely saying that we can't trust anyone, and President Kinji knew that better than we did. Marco, you're right, the Global Initiative is our number one concern, but probably not our only concern. Keep your eyes everywhere, all the time."

The group fell silent as they looked around the cave lobby, all of them imagining the area packed with suspects. Their team seemed too few in number to watch them all.

Serena addressed Marco. "Do you know anything else that could help us?"

Marco shook his head slowly. "I told you everything I know. I'll have to observe to learn more."

Serena said, "No, Marco, you need to go home now. You've already seen more than a child should ever see." She gestured at Estep. Estep snapped his fingers and an agent appeared to escort Marco out of the cave.

Serena reached out to hug Marco before he left, but he shrank from her touch. She extended her hand to him instead. He reluctantly shook it. Because his facial expression was blank it was difficult to tell if Marco was relieved or disappointed to be leaving them.

Serena resumed. "Let's run down what we know."

Beav volunteered. "We are down by three Supporters: "Dennis, Craig, and Garreth. We still have Bob, Jo, Devin, Mahesh, Kobin, Garreth, Tristan, and Luke. Marco is now on his way home, so we are down to ten of us: the eight remaining members of The Supporters, plus Mr. Speaker and myself. Serena will be up at the podium and Estep will be managing security – his team needs to be focused on security as well, so it's up to us ten to observe and profile. Ten of us inside the body of about two hundred is indeed a David and Goliath situation."

"A group is coming in right now." Serena pointed toward the narrow channel that led into the open space of the cave. "Places everyone. It's show time!"

They broke up the circle of chairs and placed them back where they belonged. Next, they strategized their seating plan. Mr. Speaker was in the direct center in row one. In row two, Bob was between the left end and the center. In row three, Luke was between the right end and the center. In row four, Beav was in the direct center. The pattern was repeated to the end of the rows.

As people filed in, Serena Wilcox Bridges gripped the podium with both hands and shifted her weight from one foot to the other. The last thing she needed was to have a fainting spell induced by standing still for too long during a stressful social situation. To distract herself from obsessing about vertigo she thought about her best friend and husband, Tom. She imagined him sitting there, smiling at her, and encouraging her to go on. She tried not to think about her missing asthma medicine.

Serena observed every person when they filtered in and when they took a seat in their designated area. President Kinji had arranged their assigned seating herself to ensure that key members of Congress were seated next to each other so that she could watch them from the podium (especially the oldest and boldest senators– the thirteen who hadn't been ruled out as suspects). Now this task was left to Serena, who didn't keep up with politics and had no idea who most of the senators were. Without any insight into their personalities or their records as lawmakers she would have to rely on her skills as a profiler. Fortunately profiling had always been one of her strengths as a private investigator.

Members of Congress who had already been cleared of traitorous activity were not invited to the Veiled Abyss party, but were watching everything via a delayed stream; the cave's environment had proved to be too challenging for streaming live feed. To transmit the stream, agents needed to route the data in relay-race fashion, by hand-delivering the data to tech agents positioned nearest to the cave exit; the only spot where they could find a signal.

Even though the tech team knew that their signal would most certainly be hacked, they weren't concerned. They had assured President Kinji that by the time anyone caught wind of what was going on it would be too late for outsiders to mobilize. The meeting would have a dedicated and secure transmission for the duration of the reading of President Kinji's speech. Everything was all set; the stream was live and running, all parties were seated (except for those who would remain standing for security purposes), and all eyes were on Serena.

21

"Let me begin by saying that I know you were all expecting to see the wise and beautiful President Ann Kinji at this podium instead of me, someone most of you have never seen before. President Kinji is recovering from an unfortunate incident that you will all be briefed on later. She will be absolutely fine and there is no cause for alarm. However, she is unable to deliver her presentation and rather than reschedule this for a later date, it is best that I deliver her speech on her behalf."

Serena held the president's speech in front of her, her hands trembling so hard that the paper made a crinkly sound amplified by the microphone. She said a silent prayer and steadied herself. No one objected to her announcement that she would fill in for President Kinji.

"Again, I'll remind you that these are President Kinji's words, not my own. I'll begin.

'Welcome to the Veiled Abyss Cave, the best gathering place for what I have in store for you. The word *Veiled* means hidden; we are at this moment hidden from the prying eyes of artificial intelligence as per my intention. The word Abyss means deep hole, and that's what we've found ourselves in.

I am'—

I'll stop here and remind you that this is President Kinji talking, not me, Serena Wilcox Bridges. I'll continue reading now.—

'issuing an Executive Order beyond anything history has ever seen.

How does an Executive Order apply to the crisis we are dealing with today? First I'll address the purpose of an Executive Order, and then I'll describe the status of what I referred to as a crisis. Finally, I will explain how my Executive Order meets our needs to resolve our national crisis.

Executive orders aid officers and agencies of the executive branch in managing operations within the federal government. Executive orders have the full force of law, and as President of the United States I have discretionary power as well as power granted directly to the Executive by the Constitution. Throughout United States history, challenges to the legal validity or justification for an Executive order have resulted in lawsuits.

I'm aware that if you do not agree that my order is a legal application of the power constitutionally granted to me you may bring forth a lawsuit, as is your legal right to do so and I wouldn't expect anything less from you. However, I'm more than willing to move forward as I am confident that the American people will find my actions to be justified, imperative, and ultimately appreciated. I am not the first American president to use an executive order to create big change.

Huge history-changing reform and large-scale policy changes have been created by executive order. Dwight D. Eisenhower used one to mandate the desegregation of public schools. Harry Truman used an Executive Order for the integration of the armed forces.

Of course not all usages of Executive Order have been full of greatness. Franklin D. Roosevelt delegated military authority to remove people from military zones, and then targeted Japanese Americans and German Americans, paving the way for Japanese-Americans to be sent to internment camps during World War II. You may well want to pay attention to what I just said about the use of military authority, as it is a hint about what is to come.

The crises I've been referring to cannot be resolved without the cooperation of Congress. Until the House and the Senate can compromise and work together we can't move forward as a nation. How many more years must we languish before we admit defeat? We have let Congress deteriorate to the point that we are now at risk of an irreversible breakdown of our entire system of government.

We need a swift response to avoid a complete and irreparable economic collapse that will devastate not only our own country, but the world markets as well. Because Congress has proven to be incapable of doing the work that they were elected by the American people to do, I must act immediately to replace them with individuals who can and *will* do the work that is urgently needed. Desperate times call for desperate measures: we are in a state of national emergency!

Therefore, I am delegating military authority to remove people from Congress. Any and all persons suspected of treason and traitorous acts will be imprisoned while awaiting trial. I will emphasize that all those arrested will receive a fair trial. I will also be clear on the following: There will be no arraignment hearing. No legal tactics that might delay or evade detainment will be tolerated. Senators, I'm giving you a Go-to-Jail card that should have been played a long time ago.'"

An audible gasp went up in the crowd- it was impressively loud, given how many collective gasps were simultaneously sputtered. Serena found this reaction to be quite satisfying. She wished Ann could have experienced it herself. Serena took a sip of water, then continued.

"I'll resume reading now. 'With the full backing of the UN, I will have temporary authority over both the House and the Senate, therefore bypassing Congress entirely. How is this possible, you might ask?

You might recall that before the Big War, we, the United States of America, freely gave up our power to the UN. We granted the United Nations power to create laws that supersede our own laws! Many Americans, including myself actually' *and by 'myself' I remind you that we are still talking about President Kinji and not me, Serena.*"

Serena paused before continuing. "'Many Americans, including myself actually, cried out that our freedom was in jeopardy. Today I am ironically using the power that we gave to the UN, to take back our power; to give authority back where it belongs, to the people. We are the people.

Congress is supposed to represent us, not rule over us. Their tyranny over the office of the presidency has rendered the Executive Branch powerless. I can't govern without a functioning Congress. American government has been deadlocked, inefficient, and unfit for so many years now that we are not only straining from the weight of tremendous debt, but we are also fast becoming morally bankrupt.

Without further ado, I will conduct the business that this gathering was created for. Members of my War Cabinet are here today, and I give them immediate authority to carry out my order, Executive Order number 03262785476. The first task at hand is to flush out those who have been involved in…' *At this point I ask that you give me, um, Serena, a second.*"

Serena sped-read through the next paragraph. Ann addressed the plot to kill her, explaining that she knew about the assassination attempt. Because the assassination had already been attempted, (unsuccessfully, thank God) shouldn't Serena skip this part? Ann also went on to question the motivation behind the attack, which was also now known, thanks to Marco's information about RDAD and the Global Initiative. Serena couldn't deliver this section of the speech as written.

Serena considered herself to be a fairly decent writer, surely she could go off script? Should she dare? She had to do something to fix this, and she had to do it now. Everyone was waiting. If the seconds dragged into minutes, the element of surprise would be long gone. Members of Congress were already chewing on the news about their impending arrest – she couldn't give them time to digest, regroup and mobilize!

It is with this logic that Serena, former private detective and mother of three, delivered a historic improvisational speech that would be truncated to sound-bites and often repeated.

"Before continuing with President Kinji's speech, I have some information of my own to deliver. President Ann Kinji knew of the assassination plot. She knew that some of you people in this very room, or rather in this cave, wanted to kill her, or more accurately were planning to have her killed, which was unsuccessful..."

Serena noticed Beav was giving her a funny look. She made a bigger effort to focus her thoughts before speaking.

"President Kinji also had an awareness that this was supposed to go down at the Global Initiative. She was on to you, so you had to step up your timetable. You tried to kill her today, but you were not successful. President Kinji will be fine. She is resting comfortably now, under the best of medical care."

Serena surveyed the shocked faces, realizing that her vantage point was the optimal position from which to observe facial reactions. Unfortunately all of them looked shocked. Were they genuinely blown away? Were some merely following the crowd; mimicking the reaction they saw in everyone else? How many of them feared Ann's Go-to-Jail card? Serena identified four people she would watch closely for the duration of her speech, four that she thought were exhibiting a fear of an impending life in prison.

"President Kinji, as I said, will recover, but the point is, the assassination attempt was real, and it did occur. We also know why it happened. We know about the RDAD agenda. An acronym for Redirect and Distract, RDAD was used to, well, redirect and distract the American people from the true agenda of the United States government."

Serena noticed a stirring in the crowd. Some of them had actually flinched at the mention of RDAD. She kept her eyes on the most agitated responders, three of whom were the same people she already had her eyes on. She let them rev up for a few seconds, then continued with her improvisational speech when their babble died down.

"For example, any issue that created polarization was a contender for RDAD. Any issue that threatened freedom was especially popular, drawing fire from both sides of the aisle, keeping the American people and Congress divided, distracted and impotent.

Issues such as gun control, abortion, marriage equality, increased government regulation over both public and private institutions; businesses, farms, schools– the list goes on—have kept Americans distracted for decades. While some, or even all, of these issues are socially and morally important, and many are human rights issues, statistics don't offer up any good case for prioritizing these issues over the larger issues that have been threatening to destroy us.

For example, let's look at the failed economy. If the economy hits a state of total collapse it affects 100% of Americans directly and all of the world population indirectly, which eventually becomes direct. What I'm trying to say is that no other issue, none of the issues pushed on us through RDAD, effects 100% of our population. While we were distracted by issues that don't carry a total-population impact, and many times not even close to that, our government kept on doing whatever it is that they were doing, which is unclear to me. My point is that we didn't demand reform because we were too busy fighting with *ourselves* about other causes.

Any time you threaten an American's freedom to make private choices, an American's freedom to defend home and family, an American's freedom to make lifestyle decisions based on religion, ethics, or personal safety, well you certainly achieve what RDAD is all about. Americans have been stepping over each other to fight for freedoms that have been denied or threatened. RDAD worked as intended.

I get it now, that RDAD was what former president John Williams must have been involved in, something he colluded about with the president before him who probably colluded with the president before *him* as well. RDAD didn't die when they did, it got stronger.

Except, RDAD lost its executive branch. You didn't trust this new President to go along with RDAD, and you are right about that. I know Ann—President Kinji—wouldn't have had any part of a program designed to deliberately mislead the American people. I know she would never subscribe to a program whose sole agenda is to create division and disharmony, to disrespect the values and beliefs of the American people by manipulating them into fighting against each other.

Anyway, you were right. She'd never go for RDAD. So you wanted to get rid of her. I know that some of you have a huge financial stake in corporations that benefit from legislation you are either preventing or pushing. I struggle to guess your motivations when you don't have financial stake in…"

Serena noticed that Beav was shaking his head and flapping his arms like a duck flying against the wind. She ignored him and kept going.

"You probably hoped that she would go away after her temporary emergency appointment post Big War, but when we elected her for an official term, in the biggest landside in history I should add, you had a problem. The American people were starting to listen to President Ann, their popular Princess. We were coming together more, and there was a glimmer of hope on the horizon that we could bridge some of the distance between the extreme left and the extreme right.

And that's exactly what you feared! The extremes are where you *want* us to be. When we are incapable of unifying, we are powerless. We spin our wheels year after year while you achieve your sneaky slimy agenda. Which is what exactly? I think I have some ideas.

The American dollar has depreciated so much that it's barely worth the paper it's printed on. We're beyond going broke, and if there's no money, there's no country. Other countries own too many of our institutions. So what happens if they call in all these debts? Foreign nations could take us over without a single shot fired. They can simply evict us. Our own government will be replaced, except maybe you snakes who are working with the foreign leaders, all members of the Global…"

Serena stopped short, noticing Beav standing and waving his arms. He gestured a director's "wrap it up" sign, a "cut" sign and some other gesture Serena had never seen before.

"Sorry, I got more off-script than I intended. My point in all of that is that we know some of you are guilty of treason. It has been established through the actions of today, of less than two hours ago. The rest of that was my own conjecture, but I stand by it. I know the evidence will bear out everything I said."

Beav vigorously shook his head. Serena made eye contact with him and shrugged. She scanned Ann's speech until she was past the section about the assassination attempt.

"Anyway, at this point I will return to President Kinji's speech." Serena removed a few pages from the stack and set them on the podium before reading the rest of Ann's speech. The crowd shuffled their feet and shifted their weight in the chairs that had grown intensely uncomfortable during their odyssey with Serena at the microphone.

"*Remember this is President Kinji talking now, not me.* 'How can I whip Congress into shape? How can I find the world leaders who have created alliances and have conspired with members of our own government to work outside the knowledge and interests of the American people?

While I was initially selected as an emergency appointment after the Big War, I stand in front of you today as your officially elected president whose first term is almost at its end.'"

Serena hesitated. *Should I be reading this part? It's too late now, I'll have to read the rest.*

She continued, "I have been your president for three years, and during all of that time, I have struggled to see through the dense fog of subterfuge and conspiracies. I ultimately became depressed, nearly despondent. I had all but given up until I understood this simple truth: I am the one person who can do something about this. I have not only the power of an Executive Order, or rather a series of several separate orders, but I also have a new power source at my disposal: the UN. And, apparently I have more friends at the UN than I thought I did because they are backing my actions unconditionally.

You see, I thought I was powerless to go up against Congress, but I was wrong. I am the one person who can make a difference. The health of the United States effects the global population. Therefore, with the full backing of the UN behind me, I have temporary emergency authority over all branches of government. With this authority I am ordering the following, effective immediately:

I hereby order, forcibly if need be, the removal of members of Congress who are known traitors.

Secondly, I order the disbandment and dissolution of the Global Oil Initiative and its parent organization, the Global Initiative.

The only way to clean house is to start over. Senators who committed treason will be immediately replaced by emergency appointees, all of whom are private citizens of upstanding character who have never had a formal association or affiliation with any political party or office.

I strongly suggest that the new Congress' first order of business be to set the term limits that have been bandied about for years. Any member of Congress whose term limits have exceeded the new regulations will be immediately placed into mandatory retirement.

The American people will later hold elections to fill the vacated congressional seats. At which time, the emergency appointees will have the option to run for office if they desire, or step down if they choose not to run. To be clear, my appointees are only temporary: the American people will elect all members of Congress as soon as we can reasonably make that happen.

Meanwhile, however, Congress will be stripped of at least three-fourths of its career politicians, due to ejection by arrest or through the new term limits regulation that I believe will pass. The majority of Congress will be flushed out and given a clean slate. There will be a period of at least thirteen months in which most of Congress will be composed of American citizens who have never held a political office. This is our best chance to have a Congress that is willing to put the needs of the American people ahead of their own.

This is the freshest start I can give you, and to create the upmost clarity in my intentions, it is imperative that I do not run for re-election."

Serena wasn't expecting Ann's speech to make such an announcement. She looked up and noticed the stunned expressions on everyone, especially those close to Ann. The transformation from surprise to sorrow was already showing on some of their faces.

She hurried to read the rest. "How can I clear Congress of its most senior politicians, stack things in my favor by appointing novices, and then run for a second term?

No, no, I will step aside for the good of the nation. It is with this in mind that I do offer you a recommendation for my replacement, someone I believe would…'"

Serena looked up from the papers she was holding with a death grip. Should she continue reading? Wasn't she over-stepping? This part could wait until President Kinji herself could deliver her speech. She had already said too much, having announced Ann's plans not to run for re-election. Why hadn't Ann warned her about what was in her speech? Serena hesitated for long enough that the crowd began to talk amongst themselves.

Serena was about to wrap things up when she detected a flurry of movement. Luke and Bob were making a beeline toward the podium.

Luke took the microphone and calmly stated, "President Kinji asked us to identify those who should be detained. I speak on behalf of my colleagues when I say that I feel certain that these persons of interest will receive a fair trial. Therefore my conscience is clear when I, and others, recite the names of those who will now be immediately arrested and escorted out of the cave, to a nearby detainment facility for interrogation and briefing."

Luke added, "We now instruct the members of Agent Estep's team, as well as members of the armed forces who are positioned just outside these cave tunnels, to arrest the following people we suspect of committing treason."

What happened next was so quiet and orderly it was dreamlike, so much so that Serena felt like everyone was in a collective trance. Bob and Luke recited four names each. As they named names, each person obediently stood up, walked down the narrow no-leg-room aisle of their seating area, and followed an agent or officer out through the cave tunnel exit.

There was not a sound beyond the soft shuffling of feet, the steady drip of the cave's ceiling over their heads, and the solemn recital of names. Each person stepped up to the microphone for their turn except for Joe. As Speaker of the House he had a conflict of interest and was advised by Dr. Kendra to refrain from comment.

Serena was next to take the podium, adding the four people she had kept an eye on during her speech; she had to point them out because she didn't know their names. Beav was next, adding seven more. The remaining Supporters named seventeen among them. When it was all said and done, thirty-six people were arrested.

All thirteen of President Kinji's

congressional suspects were confirmed as suspects. The other twenty-three persons of interest included two United States governors and members of the Global Initiative, of which ten were foreign and eleven were domestic.

But all Serena cared about at that moment was how fast she could get out of that cave, back to the surface of Planet Earth, something she could never again take for granted. The first thing she would do when she got out was take a big deep breath – minus dank, mold, bat guano, and slug. Even better than her dream of a lung-full of fresh air was seeing Tom waiting for her at the cave exit. She raced toward him until the look on his face stopped her cold.

22

Tom whisked Serena away from the mouth of the cave and led her to a waiting vehicle. An agent held the door open for them. They stepped inside and barely had time to get fully seated before the driver took off.

"You're scaring me Tom. What's going on?"

Tom cleared his throat several times, a nervous habit that alarmed Serena even more. "President Kinji took a turn for the worse after a second attempt on her life while at the hospital."

"What? Oh no! How did that happen? She was under high-levels of security!"

"They gassed the entire wing. Her security detail died trying to protect her." Tom reached across Serena's lap to hold her hand.

"Oh no, this is horrible. I can't believe it."

"They think she will pull through with no setbacks or damage."

"So you aren't saying that she's dying?"

"No." Tom looked away.

"Then what is it that you aren't telling me?"

"You didn't get news coverage while in the cave. But we got yours-- I saw you on TV and so did everyone else."

Serena tried to process what he was saying. "What do you mean?"

"The whole world knows that President Kinji has taken over the government. The reaction has been violent."

Dread settled like a ball of lead in Serena's stomach. "How violent? What's happened?"

"The kids are fine."

"What do you mean 'the kids are fine'? Why wouldn't they be fine?" Serena's panic registered in her voice. Her hand subconsciously scrabbled at the door latch, even though they were still on the road, and nowhere close to her children.

"They didn't just gas the hospital. They gassed our house too."

Serena's tongue felt like cotton in her mouth. "Our house? And you were home?"

"We were home."

Serena could hear herself ask the next question as if she was listening to her own voice from outside of her body. "Where are they?"

Tom gave her hand a squeeze. "They're at the CDC. We're headed there now."

Serena pulled her hand away. "They're fine? What do you mean fine? They are *going* to be fine, or they *are* fine? What's the level of fine?"

"They're fine. They are under observation. Do you think I'd leave them if they weren't okay? They're watching movies and eating pizza."

"You scared me. You really, really scared me. I shouldn't have put them in danger. My work for the president is over as of now."

"Hey, I said that they're okay. You'll see for yourself soon. You did good today. I watched the whole thing."

"Until you got gassed."

"Right." Tom said nothing for a few seconds before adding, "I saw most of it. You were impressive."

Serena smiled. "I could be President."

"You were."

"Yes, for a little while there I was, wasn't I?" Serena thought about that.

Tom's phone buzzed. He glanced at the number. "It's for you."

Estep's voice was so loud and abrasive that Tom could overhear everything he was saying, including the tone he was saying it in. "Where are you?"

"On my way to the CDC. My kids were…"

"I know about that. That's under control. You should be here."

"Where? The hospital?"

"The Cube. We're interrogating suspects."

"Can't it wait?"

"Gee, I don't know. Why don't we let riots build until civil war breaks out?"

"I want to see my kids first."

"I'm sending Beav. He'll brief you on the

way."

"Estep, I'm not leaving until I spend some time with my kids."

Estep disconnected the call.

Serena stayed with her family through the rest of the movie. They had saved her a slice of pizza. She didn't realize how hungry she was until she smelled the food. It felt good to eat with Tom and the kids, even though they had already eaten and all they could offer her was cold leftover fast food.

She hugged each of them multiple times when Beav turned up at the door. Tom assured her that he could hold down the fort, but Serena had already vowed that her investigative work was over. As she walked the halls of the newly built Center for Disease Control, located within a few miles of The Cube, she better understood why Ann hated The Cube. It *did* suck people in. Well, no more. Let this be a wake-up call; she would see this thing out and then she would go home – to stay.

Serena didn't think she could take any more of Estep without more food in her first. That one slice of pizza only served as an appetizer. She hadn't eaten anything else since early that morning. She could also do with some coffee. Her hunger and fatigue must have shown on her face because Beav suggested that they stop along the way.

"Estep is in a hurry for me to get there. He's in a mood."

"We need to get him a dog."

Serena agreed. "But that idea won't help us get through tonight."

"I know a friend who can make that happen."

"Beav, you always know a friend."

"She runs an animal shelter. She'll open for us."

"You mean now? We're getting him a dog now?"

"Why not? Today could have been the end, but it wasn't. We're alive. You just saw your family. And I, well, I have me. What does he have?"

They left the discussion hanging while the two of them rested in the diner that Beav had referred to as a hidden treasure. They ate together in companionable silence. When they were finished eating every crumb off their plates, which took only a matter of minutes due to their state of hunger and their hurry, he calculated a modest tip and paid the tab.

Then he took up where he left off. "Estep is never going to get out of his funk if we don't help things along. He needs a dog."

When Serena didn't come back with another rebuttal, Beav placed a call to his friend Christine. Within a half hour they were at the animal shelter. Christine greeted Beav warmly, Beav thanked her for opening the doors after-hours for him, and a quick introduction of Serena was made.

Christine then showed Serena and Beav the kennels, which were all full to maximum capacity, and beyond. A few animals were in plastic crates along the floor. Serena suspected that this practice was bending regulations. Word had apparently gotten out that the shelter had a soft spot for taking in any stray, even reptiles and—*surely that wasn't a goldfish?*

Christine led them directly to a dog that was barking for their attention. "This friendly guy is part Welsh Corgi with a mix of something else. Look how loveable he is. It breaks my heart that we haven't found a home for him yet."

Beav opened the enclosure and knelt down on the concrete slab kennel floor. The dog bounded over to him and tried to jump into his lap. Beav sat on the floor to accommodate the dog's wish. He was a big dog, taking up more than Beav's available lap space.

Serena laughed. "He sure is friendly, you're right about that."

"Aww, how can you turn this guy down? I don't think I can leave him here." Beav stood up and tried to avoid the dog's pleading eyes.

Christine moved down the row, past the cages containing kittens, cats, and an obese rabbit.

"Ooh, what a beautiful dog!" Serena stopped in front of a kennel that Christine had passed by.

"Roxy is a Jack Russell. I'm watching him for my friend Marie. She'd be upset with me if I gave her dog away! But I offer you this handsome German Shepherd."

"A Shepherd does sound like a good fit for Agent Estep."

Christine said, "We're so fond of Finn. I'd keep him myself if I didn't already have too many animals. He was a service dog."

Serena clasped her hands together, a gesture which made both dogs' ears perk up. "Yes! He's perfect. Estep needs a highly trained, highly disciplined dog."

Beav couldn't let go. "How is a highly trained dog better than this loveable mutt I have right here?"

Serena groaned. "Because Estep will be a tough sell. The service training issue will help."

They both looked at the German Shepherd. Finn certainly did have a noble quality. He tilted his head and looked at them with his kind soulful eyes. Oh yes, Estep would most definitely fall in love with this dog. They had nothing to worry about.

"We'll take him," said Serena.

Beav dragged his feet. "And him too." He pointed at the friendly mutt with the wild eyes and the tongue hanging out of a big toothy grin.

Christine's face lit up. "You want both dogs?"

Beav had made up his mind. "I can't leave him here. He's coming home with me. You like that, don't you, Toby?" The dog barked happily as if on cue.

Serena asked Christine, "Do you name all the animals as they come in?"

Beav laughed. "I named him when he jumped into my lap."

The animal shelter visit took less than ten minutes and created a rift between them and their unsuspecting driver. And when those minutes were added to the time they spent at the diner, and the extra drive time spent getting on and off the freeway twice, they were almost an hour behind schedule.

With no time to figure out a better plan they put both dogs in the backseat together. Serena was worried that the dogs wouldn't react well to that situation, but Beav was confident that the two fellows would get along splendidly. Beav was right. By the end of the trip, Toby had fallen asleep with his head on good-natured Finn's back. Finn, awake and alert for the entire trip, seemed to watch over Toby.

"Aww, look at that," said Beav.

Serena was quick to say, "You can't keep both dogs!"

"I know, I know. Let's get Finn to Estep

before I lose my willpower. I'm having doubts that he will be good to this dog."

"Oh come on, you know he will be. It won't take him long and he'll be asking me to knit sweaters for Finn."

Beav was astonished. "You knit?"

"Theoretically he might ask me to knit a doggie sweater. And if I knew how to knit I would do it."

"HA! I didn't think that sounded right."

The two chatted about nothing important while the driver grudgingly took them where they wanted to go. Their next stop was to drop Toby off at Beav's friends' house. The Sharot family was available at this hour to take Toby, and they did live nearby, but this pit stop added even more delay to their already tardy arrival. Serena had grown anxious and had already checked in several times for updates about what was going on with the investigation.

Finally they arrived at The Cube. They brought Finn with them, with no plan for how to smuggle him in. Serena regretted the impulsive decision to get Estep a dog; but because Finn was a German Shepherd, no one even asked why they had a dog with them. It was shockingly easy to sneak an unauthorized dog into The Cube.

Of course security was lax because they had access to the private back entrance. If they had tried the standard employee corridor, or worse yet the public access entrance, they wouldn't have gotten Finn past the first checkpoint.

However, being on the super-secret covert team had its perks, and this was one of them. They trotted Finn all the way to the conference room where Estep was already in a mood – this dog was absolutely necessary. Their plan could go either way, but looking again into Finn's beautiful eyes, Serena couldn't imagine how it could go wrong.

When Estep saw Finn he stopped dead in his tracks. Whatever he was in the middle of saying would remain forever unsaid. He was slack-jawed and speechless, for about two seconds. "That thing better not have anything to do with me."

"That *thing* is a dog, *your* dog," said Beav.

"I don't have a dog. I *won't* have a dog."

Serena threw something directly at Estep's

feet.

Estep flinched and yelled, "What the--!"

Finn shot over to Estep in a flash. He scooped up the object and obediently sat directly in front of Estep as if waiting for a command. Estep studied him. He said, "Drop."

Finn released the object.

Estep picked it up – a sticky peanut-buttery ball, a canine treat that Christine had given Serena for Finn. Finn watched Estep take the treat away. Estep muttered to himself and threw the treat. Finn retrieved it and returned to where Estep was standing. Estep tried the command a second time. "Drop."

Finn obeyed.

Estep patted Finn's head. "Good boy."

Finn tilted his head.

"It's yours."

Finn picked up the treat, lay down, and settled in for a good chew.

Estep turned toward Beav and Serena. He ignored their self-righteous expressions and said, "You're late."

Serena said, "His name is Finn."

Estep admired his new best friend. He was so

impressed with Finn that his hostile obsession with his ex-girlfriend felt far behind him. He didn't even care that Serena and Beav were acting superior. In fact, he could even admit that he was grateful that they had pushed this dog on him.

Best of all, Finn was already generating impressive results as an anger management therapy dog for Estep. When Estep brought Serena back to the interrogation room he made no further mention of the fact that she was over an hour late. Incredibly he didn't utter a single snarky remark during the entire two minute walk through the maze of corridors.

The Cube had never been a holding place for criminals. However, government insiders arrested for treason were a different breed of criminal and due to the extreme situation at hand, and the sheer number of individuals involved, the judgment call was made to conduct the interrogation just a few doors down from President Kinji's office.

An entire wing of The Cube watched the proceedings from the peanut gallery in the conference room. With no two-way mirror in their makeshift interrogation room, they watched the interrogation via a live feed on multiple screens. Serena, Estep and Beav observed the interrogation from a separate room with a few other investigators and profilers. They too watched from a live feed. None of the signal problems existed in The Cube that had challenged the tech support team at the cave earlier that same day, but with all personnel tapped out and sleep deprived even a routine job was taxing.

The late hour, now pressing toward midnight, did nothing to deter the media from camping out on The Cube's lawn. The media circus was definitely in full swing, and the American people had also begun to gather. By morning Chicago would be a powder keg for riots and all manner of chaos. Chicago's finest had already stepped up their patrols and had assembled their best teams. Security teams that normally scheduled high-profile events at least a year in advance were forced to coordinate full-scale security of the nation's new capital with merely a few minutes' notice.

Serena addressed Estep. "I'm still not clear

on why the interrogations are being held here instead of at the agency or at the prison. This is crazy!"

Estep nodded. "I can't believe I'm saying this, but I agree with you. President Kinji insists that there is no place more secure than The Cube. More importantly, she wants every word witnessed by as many in government as possible, and the best way to do that, she says, is to bring the traitors directly to the government. By the way, if any of those witnesses want to go into the interrogation room itself we are to escort them in. Can you imagine? So far no one has asked. Then again, I didn't tell them that they have the option. I figure I had leeway to make a judgment call."

Serena asked, "How is President Ann doing?"

Estep snorted. "She's fit to be tied that they won't let her out of bed yet. She was online with me as soon as she came to."

Serena laughed. "That sounds like her. What a relief, huh? This has been a harrowing journey."

"Yes." Estep answered in one syllable.

With a break in the interrogation, and nothing to watch on the feed, there was no reason why their conversation couldn't continue. Serena prattled on. "I can't imagine keeping that woman down under normal circumstances. The nation is a circus and she's stuck in a hospital. She must be going out of her mind. I bet she's giving Ted a hard time."

Estep raised his eyebrows. The conversation was becoming too chatty; he wasn't Serena's gal pal. He was about to make a snarky remark when his eyes rested upon Finn's silhouette. *What a fine dog.* Estep forgot what he was planning to say.

Serena followed his gaze. "Ah, yes, Finn. I almost forgot about him. He's been so quiet."

"Hey, what's that he's got?" Estep moved in closer.

"That's my inhaler! I see my name on the label – look!" Serena bounced up and down like a child on Christmas morning. "Get it from him! That's our missing link!"

Estep instructed, "Finn, Drop!"

Finn walked directly to Estep and dropped the inhaler at his feet.

Estep took a cloth from his pocket and used it to pick up the inhaler. He turned it over to read the label. "It's yours. What do you mean by missing link?"

Serena explained. "We know who attempted the Plan B attack on President Kinji in the cave. It was obvious because it happened right in front of us. But who else was behind it? I can't imagine that all of the members of the conspiracy, the many layers of it, are all accounted for. We need the link to the others, especially the ones still here in The Cube. And this is it. When we find out where Finn got that from we'll have our missing link."

Finn's movement had caught Beav's attention. He ambled over to where Estep and Serena were standing quietly, staring at the dog. Beav said, "The question is, how do we get Finn to tell us where he found the inhaler?"

Serena shrugged. "I don't think we can do that, but we can figure it out ourselves. Find his treat and you'll know where he's been."

Estep didn't find the treat itself but an askew grate caught his eye. He moved the grate, a heater cover with missing screws, with his foot.

Finn's treat was resting on the heating duct. "How much you want to bet that Finn dropped his treat in there, and found the inhaler when he tried to retrieve it?"

Serena solved the mystery aloud. "The inhaler switch was made outside of the cave, when my purse was briefly left unattended in the car. We can assume that someone went back to this room after the switch was made. That doesn't make sense. Why not toss my inhaler into a Dumpster? Hiding it here is absurd. So we can surmise that this hiding place wasn't intentional. He or she removed the grate screws and dropped it in the heating duct because there was no opportunity to get rid of it elsewhere."

Serena pondered that for a second before saying, "Where are the screws?"

Beav noticed the feed was back up. "They're starting back up again."

Serena shook her head. "This is more pressing. You go watch. Agent Estep and I should focus on this. Buzz me if I miss anything important."

Beav gave her a thumbs up and re-joined the group gathered in front of the feed screens.

Estep and Serena searched every desk drawer, every trash bin, and every pencil holder they could find. They searched under desks, chairs and tables. They searched under seat cushions. "If he shoved the screws into his pocket, they won't be in this room," said Estep.

"We're assuming that this is a man? That's my gut feeling too I suppose. If he was antsy to get the inhaler off of his person, why would he then keep the screws? No, they are here. We have to keep looking," Serena insisted.

Estep examined the ceiling tiles for any sign that one of the tiles had been moved. He looked at the light fixtures and the beams.

Serena was a bit too short to easily reach the window sills, but she slid her hand along the sills over her head. She found nothing but dust on the first two window sills she tried. When she hit the third window sill, the one nearest to the grate, she was rewarded with a tell-tale sound of metallic clinking when the screws hit a metal desk near the window.

"Now what? This doesn't tell us anything." Estep said.

"It confirms that someone deliberately

removed the screws to hide the inhaler in there. We were right about where Finn found the inhaler. That being confirmed, if the person who hid the inhaler didn't wear gloves, we should be able to get an ID from the screws or the inhaler."

Estep pointed out, "The inhaler has dog slobber on it. We might not be able to pull anything usable off of that."

"But the screws don't. We have lab tech on emergency call."

Estep scowled at her. "Yes, I know, I set that up." Finn sat at attention when Estep's tone of voice changed. Estep noticed this and when he spoke again it was without the abrasive tone that Finn had reacted to. "Finding the screws is a good lead, good job."

Serena glanced at Finn and smiled. She whispered, "Thanks, buddy."

Estep called the lab team. They arrived in under two minutes, beating their personal best drill response time. They tested the screws and Serena's inhaler. They confirmed that the inhaler at the cave had been used to transport the powder. The powder residue proved beyond a shadow of a doubt that this was the plastic casing used to carry the toxin into the cave. If they could lift prints from Serena's inhaler or the screws, they would have the connection they needed – the evidence to link the two inhalers, the assassination attempt to someone at The Cube, and probably additional people after following known associations to the person they were hopefully about to catch red-handed.

The worrisome part of this is that the person who hid the inhaler must have been present at the cave. There hadn't been an opportunity for a known suspect to hide the inhaler because all suspects were immediately detained. There was no other explanation; someone who should have been marked for detainment had slipped through the cracks and had then gone straight to The Cube. Serena picked her brain for anything that she may have forgotten about. *How could she have missed this? Who was it?*

The interrogation had hit another lull and Beav had wandered back to where Serena and Estep were. He had watched the lab crew with great interest. "Don't worry. If the prints are there, we've got him so jammed he's ready for toast. The lab team used a scanning Kelvin probe fingerprinting technique. It makes no physical contact with the print and there's no use of developers. Fingerprints are recorded while leaving intact material we'll put through DNA analysis later to confirm the results."

Serena stared at him, "What are you talking about?"

Beav clarified, "Rest assured, if the prints are there, we can make a solid irrefutable identification from them. We'll have a tentative ID right away. I give them all of fifteen minutes and they'll be back here with a name. Because whoever it is, they are obviously in the system."

"I don't care who it is anymore. I'm too tired to think. I want to go home."

Beav clamped a hand on Serena's shoulder. "Sometimes it's better not to think aloud."

23

Mr. Speaker Joseph Smythe was not in The Cube. He was discouraged from attending due to President Kinji's hospitalization. While Vice President Lehman had everything under control and was technically the acting President of the United States, it was Joe who they relied upon to keep America running while Ann was recuperating. The inner workings of the government didn't stop because a sensational situation was ablaze at The Cube. No, someone needed to be at the wheel of the old grind. Between he and Lehman, the nation would run as usual in most areas of government. Regardless of what was going on at The Cube tonight, a mundane yet grueling schedule was on his plate for tomorrow. There was nothing to be gained from watching the play-by-play on social media at 1:00AM.

Joe had drifted off to sleep when his intercom system buzzed. "Who could it be at this hour?" His stomach tightened, knowing that the answer couldn't possibly bring good news.

Joe was not a good fighter. He intimated people with his confident persona, but the truth was, if he was ever pressed into action he wasn't of much use defending himself or others. Because of this, he brought the nearest thing to a weapon that he saw; a rubber mallet he had recently used to pound a wooden leg back into a kitchen stool that had fallen apart.

"Yes?" he said through the intercom.

"It's me, Jo." Her voice was garbled but still recognizable.

"Irish Jo?"

"You know a lot of Jo's do you?"

"No, only you."

"Will you let me in now please?"

"Oh of course," he said into the intercom, realizing too late that yet another word via the intercom was ridiculous when he could have simply opened the door. He was still holding the rubber mallet when Jo walked over the threshold.

She smirked.

Joe followed her gaze to the rubber mallet in his hand and gave himself a mental head slap. "I didn't know who would be at the door at this hour."

"Clearly. I could have been a mole."

"Please don't even joke about being a spy."

"I wasn't. I meant as in 'Whack-a-mole'." She gestured at the mallet.

"Oh, ha. Yeah, funny." Joe tossed the mallet on the sofa, barely missing hitting the lamp on the side table. "What brings you here in the middle of the night?"

Not that he minded. He admired her red hair, and the way it curled down her back. When she moved her locks bounced off her body. He contemplated this for much longer than he realized. Joe ran his hands over his face and analyzed his intentions. *What am I doing? How could flirting be appropriate during a time of national crisis? I'm the Speaker of the House, not your average Joe – Get a grip, Joe, get a grip!* Hadn't he disgraced himself enough with the show he put on in the Veiled Abyss?

The story of Joe bumbling through a row of chairs, inadvertently giving terrorists the diversion that they needed to assemble a weapon, had hit the Social Media Channel news just before midnight. The media lifted an image from video feed that they had somehow obtained from the tech team – Joe made a mental note to find out how that happened. The chair incident occurred before the public broadcast, yet the media had gotten hold of it and was looping Joe's bumbling-chair buffoonery.

"Tell me why you're here," he tried again. This time he kept his eyes above her neckline, which was cut distractingly low.

"I'm here because I think I know something. It occurs to me that I don't believe Luke."

Joe struggled to remember who Luke was. Of course, he headed up The Supporters. Yes, he knew Luke; Luke was the one who Joe had, in his private thoughts, renamed as 'the punk kid'. "They vetted all of you, so I've been told. How could they get it so wrong? Are you sure?"

"No, I don't mean that Luke is a traitor. But I do think that he is covering for someone else. Luke's behavior hasn't always added up." Jo twirled a curl with her finger, a nervous habit that was driving Joe wild.

"This won't wait until morning because…?" Joe couldn't stay on the straight and narrow for long. She needed to get to the point fast.

"Because if I'm right, you guys missed a suspect. He's probably at The Cube right now. The conspirators are losing, and time is running out. They have nothing left to lose – that's a dangerous situation for anyone who is in the vicinity when they pull their next stunt."

"I understand, but President Kinji is still hospitalized. They did attempt to kill her there, as you are probably aware of, and while they did take out her security detail, they didn't cause her any real harm. She's under even more security now. Point is, she's not at The Cube, so what are you suggesting?"

"I don't know. I think the plan might be terrorism in general, not necessarily with President Kinji as their target. If The Cube were destroyed, or at least partially destroyed, all while the president is also hospitalized, wouldn't it be enough to tip the scales into chaos? The nation is already on the brink. Don't they keep you informed? Haven't you at least been watching the news? Americans are ready to do themselves in with violent and lunatic mayhem. A country can only take so much disruption before all hell breaks loose."

"Hold on, I've only been home for about forty-five minutes at the most. Yeah, they keep me informed." Joe laughed. *Flirting again, stop it!* "Yes, you could be right about terrorism. I'm taking you seriously. I don't know what I can do though. Unless you know who to look for specifically, there's nothing new to report. They're already on high alert at The Cube. Honestly, I don't know why you felt the need to come here. This could have kept until morning."

"I know who to look for."

Joe blinked, startled. "Then stop playing around and tell me." He was ashamed of himself for flirting and delaying her message.

"They need to take a long look at Kevin Port."

"Kevin Port? I've never heard of him."

"He worked with Governor Carson Landon. He was a friend of Luke's. I'm realizing now that he was probably spying for The Supporters. But can anyone trust him? Kevin's probably been playing both sides all along!"

"Do you have any proof?"

"I remember something that Luke had let slip when Carson died. He said 'I hope Carson didn't tell them anything.' He was worried that before Carson did himself in, he may have talked. About what?"

"I don't know. I can ask that the team look into Kevin Porch."

"Port. It's Kevin Port."

"Isn't that what I said?"

"No, you said Kevin Porch." The name Kevin Porch struck her funny bone. Maybe it was the lack of sleep, but she was struggling not to break into hysterics. Yes, she must be hitting delirium, she thought. *Kevin Porch won't seem funny after I get some sleep.*

"I'll call right now. Stay here and listen." Joe made the call, and he was careful to get the name right: Kevin Port.

"I feel better now, thank you." Jo looked up at Joe, and wondered how urgent her message really was. Had she somehow invented the crisis as an excuse to come over? Was she really that much of a basket case? Yes, maybe she was. The thought of going back to her empty apartment after everything that happened in the cave was hard to stomach.

The more she thought about it, the more Jo wondered if there was nothing to this sudden insight into a suspect, nothing but her imagination inventing a reason to see Joe. She twirled her hair with her pinky finger and brooded. She didn't realize that she was staring up at him for so long that he mistook her preoccupation with his face as a signal, as permission.

He held her face with both of his hands and leaned in to kiss her. His lips lightly brushed hers before she reacted to his touch by jumping backwards as if she was bitten by a snake, kissed by a toad, or something equally hideous. Joe responded by saying the first thing that popped into his head. "No offense."

Jo's face flushed a brilliant magenta. "No offense? You should be offended, Joe. I'm so sorry. I didn't mean to—you startled me. I didn't expect—oh come here!" Jo pulled him close to her by tugging on the collar of his shirt, the pale yellow dress shirt he hadn't bothered to change out of. When his face was close to hers, she looked into his eyes. She hesitated only slightly.

Joe didn't need any more encouragement than this. He kissed her again, and this time she received his kiss, for a long time. Minutes passed. Neither of them knew how many. When they finally stopped for a breather they suddenly felt as if they needed to know everything there was to know about each other right now, all at once. Joe moved the rubber mallet off the couch and they sat there, gazing into each other's eyes and chatting all night long.

They were still sitting there together as dawn approached and Joe's phone buzzed. Jo heard his side of the conversation:

"Yes, I see."

"No, Kevin Porch was only a possibility."

"Yes, that's who I meant, Kevin Port."

"I know, I said 'Porch'. I did mean Port."

"I understand. I was following a tip."

"No, I don't want to pursue it further. I understand what you meant by 'he had an alibi'."

"No, I don't want to place a formal inquiry since you already informed me that he is not a viable suspect."

"Yes, actually I do have another concern. It's not about Kevin Por-"

Jo whispered "Port."

"It's not about Kevin Port. It's about footage airing on the Social Media Channel."

"Yes, I'm talking about the chair footage." Joe snapped.

Jo giggled.

"Yes, that's the one. How did they get it?"

"Oh, I see. I didn't know that those were released."

"I want to know if you can zoom in on the part where I'm, um, not tripping on the chairs."

"Yes, the background."

"Right. Can you do it?"

"You're looking for anyone who isn't

watching me tripping on the chairs."

"Very funny, everyone was watching, right. Whoever wasn't watching was assembling a weapon."

"Yes, you idiot, *that* weapon."

24

"Nicholas, what are you doing here?" Serena rushed over to him, her arms outstretched.

"Ms. Wilcox, you do a lot of hugging," he said, while allowing himself to be squeezed. The zipper pull on Serena's leather jacket scratched his check when he pulled away.

Estep answered, "The lab tech guys are wearing down. They're calling everyone in."

"Maybe you'll help us solve the case. We

have them working on lifting prints," said Serena.

"No, I don't think so. They put me on database duty." Nicholas was taken aback by something he saw out of the corner of his eye. "Hey, what's he doing here?"

Serena looked around her, startled. No one else was around. "Who?"

"That guy who just left. I know him from Clyde's computer lab. We worked on the Angels Mark technology together."

Serena raised her eyebrows. "Oh? Is he an old friend of yours?"

Nicholas scowled. "He's a liar and a thief."

The hair on Serena's arms rose—goose bumps. "What was he stealing?"

"He was selling my work. Clyde caught him and kicked him out of the program."

"Your work on Angels Mark?"

"Yes."

"What could it do? Besides the way Paul wanted to use it, could it do more?"

Nicholas nodded. "It could do a lot more! It could track the Internet history of hundreds of users simultaneously. It could block searches too."

"Who did he sell it to?" Serena saw that Estep and Beav were starting to pay attention to their conversation. She held her finger to her lips. They kept a respectful distance, allowing Serena to question Nicholas without interruption.

"Paul Tracy said that he was selling to someone who works for the president. Not President Kinji, the dead one."

"President John Williams?" Serena's pulse raced. *Could it be that pieces of the puzzle that had been missing for years were finally starting to come together?*

"Yes."

"Nicholas, remember how frustrated you were when President Kinji's office was hacked? I think you were fighting against your own genius. That was Angels Mark technology, I'd bet on it."

Nicholas tugged at his Superman shirt, cracked his knuckles, and ran his hand through his hair. "I think you're right. I was fighting against myself."

"Bizarro, huh?"

"Yeah, I guess so. I know how to remove the hack now. Thank you, Ms. Wilcox."

"Your friend…" Serena made eye contact with Estep. She tapped her wrist where a watch would have been had she been wearing one. Estep nodded and signaled an alert to his team.

"He's not my friend."

"This guy you worked with, do you know his name?"

"Luke Halloway."

Commotion erupted as Estep took off running down the corridor. His team was strategically placed throughout the entire wing of The Cube so that there was no way that Luke could slip past them. Serena wanted to see the take-down for herself. Apparently so did Beav because he sprinted after Estep, soon overtaking him.

Serena never ran anywhere unless she was being chased by something, so she didn't venture any further out than the next room over. As fate would have it, the next room over was where Luke was. Serena saw him before he saw her. She whispered to Nicholas, "Go back!" Then she added, "And call Estep."

Serena made sure that Nicholas left before she crept deeper into the room, hiding behind bookcases. The space was a dedicated study and library area, for browsing records or for leisure reading. What Luke was doing there was a mystery that soon became clear. He was leaving a message for someone by putting a piece of paper into a book and then returning it to the shelf where he got it from. When he turned around, Serena was standing there, a few inches from his face.

"You're taller," he said.

"I'm wearing boots."

"I suppose those gorillas in the hall are looking for me."

"I suppose so." Serena knew that Luke couldn't have gotten past security with a weapon, and she was fairly confident that if put to the test she could take him. Someone needed to give this kid a hamburger—and let him outside more often.

Luke apparently thought more of his own physical strength and abilities than Serena did because he leaned into Serena's personal space and gave her a shove.

"You pushed me!" Serena grabbed Luke by the collar of his hoodie and pulled him close to her. "I have to warn you that I'm a hugger." She snatched him up and managed to turn him around. Holding him with his back against her chest, and grateful for the leather jacket barrier between the two of them, she locked her arms into a physical hold.

Luke thrashed around, swore, and flung his legs back to kick her in the shins.

Before now, she was physical with Luke only to restrain him, but the pain sparked her temper. The sharp pain of his shoe on her leg caused her to lash out and slap his face. Serena's slap left a handprint.

Estep and Beav rushed into the reading room at that instant. Upon seeing the handprint on Luke's face, both men burst out laughing. Luke glowered and jerked his body around as he was dragged off in handcuffs while being serenaded by laughter. It was only after Estep was crying and Beav had the hiccups that the two men finally composed themselves.

Meanwhile, Serena hadn't left the reading room. She removed the book she had seen Luke put the message in: there it was! The paper was incriminating indeed. It said, "Dead man can't talk. Paul's gone. I want my money."

She ran down the corridor, realizing that she was willing to run for a good cause. "Wait, wait!"

The two agents who held Luke's cuffed arms stopped.

Serena triumphantly raised the note above her head. "Recognize this? We have you for treason and murder. Anything you want to say to help yourself?"

Luke said nothing.

Serena tried again. "Who hired you? Who is the message for? You have nothing left to lose. You're under twenty-one. The judge may be able to award you protective custody in prison, if he's feeling charitable."

Everyone in the corridor held their breath waiting for Luke to speak. Beav had the presence of mind to initiate the video function on his phone to record Luke's confession. Estep quickly read Luke his rights, even though that routine was likely unnecessary given that Luke was a terrorist. Even so, there was no room for error in this investigation. With their I's dotted and their T's crossed, they were ready to listen to what Luke had to say.

"I worked for President William's administration. When he died, nothing really changed. I kept on giving them what they wanted. They didn't have Williams anymore, but they still had control of the Global Initiative. I've told you everything. Give me an offer for protection—in writing."

Serena put her finger over her mouth and maintained a thinking pose before saying, "I'll talk to the judge for you. I'll tell him how your actions put some of my favorite people in danger, including myself. And I'll tell him that when you were cornered by a weapon-less five-foot-two middle aged woman you kicked her in the shin."

25

Lehman shielded his eyes to see past the glare of the stage lights. "Is that you, Serena?"

"Yes, I'm here with Agent Estep."

Lehman hopped down from the stage and invited Serena and Estep to sit. They were alone in the convention hall, an audience of three facing an empty stage. Within the hour the room would be filled to capacity to hear Lehman's address.

"Does it seem funny to have me on the other

side of this?" Lehman asked.

Serena thought about it. "No, not really. You've always had a leadership quality about you. Do you plan to run for office?"

Lehman shook his head. "My wife and I bought a house in Texas. As thrilling as it is to temporarily act as President, I don't want to be in this role, or in the role of Vice President either. When President Kinji is back on her feet I'll ask her to find a replacement for me. I'm going home."

"I wish you all the best. I've enjoyed working with you sir," said Agent Estep.

Lehman nodded. "I don't have much time to talk before things get busy. I want to run down what we know. Please stop me if I get something wrong. The people behind this were part of the Global Initiative, and that's the connection to foreign interests. The financial take-over had been in the works for over twenty years, even further back than that for some key properties. It's fairly obvious what the motivation was regarding other countries wanting to take us down, buy us out, and take us over. It's the usual subjects as far as foreign terror is concerned – no surprises."

Serena confirmed, "Yes, you've got it right so far."

Lehman asked, "The other handle communicating with Carson Landon through the crack in the media channel- was it foreign or domestic?"

Serena leaned her head back and let herself sink into the chair. She closed her eyes. "Foreign. None of that seems important now. We can easily bust that up, especially with the help of the UN. The UN will give President Kinji whatever she wants, for as long as the health of the United States economy is in dire straits."

Lehman continued, "There's no single enemy here. There's no one person to blame. Covert Coffee has led us to multiple persons and groups who wanted to sabotage President Kinji's administration and even wanted her taken out of office entirely by way of assassination, of which there were multiple plots and two actual attempts that resulted in serious injury to the President."

When Lehman paused, Estep said, "Correct."

Lehman went on, "No one will be surprised that foreign nations were involved, and their identities will be of no surprise either, as they are the typical suspects. It's no shocker that Congress was working against President Kinji, but I am blown away by how deep the traitorous activity went and how far-flung it was. I can accept that we won't have one villain to pin everything on. Few things in life have tidy resolutions. I do need to offer somebody up though. Americans are going to want a name and a face."

Serena sat up straight. "Give them the person who was directly responsible for assembling the weapon that nearly killed President Kinji."

Lehman flipped through his notecards. He chose to use actual paper cards because he felt more in control over his public speaking experience when holding his words in his hands. There was something about reading from a screen that made him feel anxious. He couldn't find any reference to what Serena was talking about in his notes. "Have they released that name yet?"

Serena said, "I don't know, have they?"

Agent Estep answered, "I don't think so, but it's solid. We have him in custody."

Serena explained, "You can offer up the three men from The Supporters who were involved in the assassination attempt in the cave: Dennis, Craig, and Garreth. Those three were caught in the act with too many witnesses for them to stand any chance of getting away with it. They were arrested immediately and removed from the cave. We went on the best that we could. We identified many other suspects but one of The Supporters involved in the assassination attempt slipped through the cracks."

Estep added, "Serena's inhaler was used to bring the toxin into the cave. The man who masterminded the attack walked right back out of the cave with it. It was only after we found the inhaler at The Cube that we were able to identify the subject."

Lehman addressed his comment to Estep, "I heard that it was your dog Finn who found the evidence. People love animal hero stories, that's good for me to put into my address."

Serena continued, "After the identification came through we were able to cross reference it with video footage from the video stream the tech team had at the cave. When the Speaker of the House…"

"Tripped over the chairs?" Lehman guessed.

Serena nodded. "When he tripped over the stairs The Supporters used that distraction to assemble the weapon. So, between the inhaler found at The Cube and the video footage we have absolute proof of his involvement."

"Who's involvement?" asked Lehman, his pen ready.

"Luke." Serena looked down at her feet.

"The leader of The Supporters?" Lehman asked.

Serena confirmed, "Yes, he was a double agent. He fooled everyone. Bob is in charge of The Supporters now. It really is a good group of citizen watchdogs—they aren't a militia or even vigilantes in the true sense of the word. Ninety-nine percent of them are law-abiding citizens who only want to protect America from corrupt government through knowledge; not through violence, hacking, spying or anything else that is illegal or treasonous. Unfortunately a lot of people were betrayed by Luke and have left The

Supporters. Jo was so humiliated by this experience that she went back to Ireland."

"Joe's Jo?" asked Lehman.

"Sadly, yes."

Lehman patted Serena's shoulder. "Hey, you have nothing to be ashamed of. You and everyone else did a beautiful job. The layers of conspiracy were from the world's biggest onion. Don't worry, I'm not going to paint an ugly picture of The Supporters. To help repair their image, I'll invite Bob to participate in the press conference following the address. He can handle any questions about the group."

Serena brightened. "That's an excellent idea!"

Lehman asked, "Is there anything else I should know about?"

Serena mulled it over. "You might want to talk about what happened when President Kinji shut the Internet down for five hours."

Lehman laughed, "Oh they'll bring it up during the press conference, no doubt. I won't help them get to it sooner. That was an awful mess, wasn't it? It was effective in cutting communications to bring down the Global

Initiative, but President Kinji had no idea how badly Americans would react to having no Internet or wireless service for just a few short hours. She was also apparently unaware how much of a snarl it would cause in the economy."

Estep said, "They're calling it Dark Tuesday."

Lehman agreed, "I've heard that too. Yes, it was a horrible day. It achieved its objective though; the nation was headed for ruin and the Global Initiative had to be shut down. Best to take the bull by the horns, which is what I'll say in defense of the decision to block communications for a few hours. The damage was horrific though. The Red Cross is still helping people recover from disasters that could have been prevented if people had had use of cell towers. I guess it wasn't such a brilliant idea for most of the country to get rid of private landlines and public pay phones."

Serena stood up and Estep followed suit. Lehman also rose. Serena said, "Good luck, Lehman. If I were you I'd spend as much time as possible talking about Finn."

26

Ann had requested a quick meeting with Serena in the VIP box before delivering her final speech to the nation. "I can't thank you enough for everything you've done."

"Of course." She saw Ann not as President, but as a friend in need of a hug. She offered her a hug now and Ann readily accepted.

When Ann broke away she wiped a tear from her eye. "It's been a long journey."

"Yes, it has. And we almost lost you."

"We almost lost *you*. You used up a few of your nine lives."

Serena shrugged. "I came away without a scratch. You're the one who was hospitalized on and off for six weeks."

"Lehman and Joe did an amazing job holding down the fort while I was down for the count. And I can't be happier with how the new Congress has been faring with so many private citizens taking on congressional seats. They did vote for term limits, did you hear?"

"Yes, I did. I'm pleased that you appointed Bob from The Supporters."

"Oh, he's been brilliant. And he has the gift of gab, being a career radio host."

"From Indiana, right? That's where Beav met him."

"No, he's from Wisconsin. He was only in Indiana for a short term assignment."

Serena laughed. "I'm remembering how Beav told me that he trusted Bob because he studied his home environment, his family pictures, and even his little dog."

"None of those things were his, no." Ann laughed too. "I'm going to miss this."

Serena shook her head. "No you won't. You're ready to move on."

"I suppose you're right."

"To be honest with you, I hate politics."

"Then why have you been a part of this for so long? You've been with me from the beginning."

"The nation has been obsessed and negative for so long that our media, our entertainment industry, our music, our social interactions, and even our cartoons are steeped in it. When people share a common misery there's no escaping it. Everyone's talking about it, everywhere. Since I can't get away from it I may as well try to help."

Ann ignored Serena's rant. She asked, "Do you remember something you told me about religion and politics?"

Serena drew a blank.

Ann refreshed her memory. "I said, 'Religion and politics don't mix.' And you came back with 'Religion and politics are always conjoined. Trying to separate the two gives us a fractured nation; one half without a heart and the other without a brain'."

"I said that? That seems wiser than my usual

rantings."

"You also said that you are 'an independent and an idealist'. Do you still feel that way?"

Serena nodded. "Oh I'll never align myself with the left or the right. I avoid extremes."

"No, I mean, do you still see yourself as an idealist."

Serena noted that Ann was watching her intently. "What's this about?"

"I have a job proposal for you."

"What kind of job proposal?"

"Listen to my speech."

Serena started to say, "Of course I will," but Ann had already left for the stage.

At the podium, President Kinji commanded respect. Her eyes reflected unmistakable intelligence, her stance projected confidence. Her natural beauty and humor were the scale-tipping ingredients that won America's hearts. They hung on every word she said because she was a celebrity, but today they listened to her for reasons beyond her charisma and popular appeal; today they needed her to be their president.

"Dear Americans, I know you are saddened by the news that I will not be running for re-election. I know that many of you believe that I've only scratched the surface of the work that needs to be done. And I agree. But I am recommending an amazing leader to take my place. You'll find that Speaker of the House Joseph Smythe is a warm and wonderful human being, with quick wit, an engaging sense of humor, and an incredible work ethic. Most importantly, given all that we've gone through, the Speaker is honest. Joe has become one of my dearest friends; I trust him wholeheartedly and I can't say enough good things about him. If anyone can move our nation forward in the right direction, it's Joe.

He will lead you into better days, times of prosperity and freedom, days that will remind you of the old America that your great-grandparents remember. I ask that you trust me and vote Joe into office. I will sleep better at night if I leave you in his hands.

And of course, I can't leave you without giving you my final thoughts, which are substantial. I dearly hope that you are listening, and that you take what I say to heart. It is my wish that my words be my legacy to this nation, and to you.

Please don't allow the bitterness and division of the past to creep back in. Don't allow government to hold that power over you, to distract you from your own ability to reason for yourself. There are big issues that have never been resolved, and will never be resolved.

When issues become more important than people, more important than truth, and more important than love – how can we justify the fight? Without mutual respect, and even support, the two will negate each other. And all that will remain is a dark void that quickly fills with anger, resentment and a house so divided that it collapses in on itself.

If you want change, you must stop doing what's always been done. Shouting to be heard above the noise merely creates more noise. You cannot win this battle: you cannot change your neighbor's point of view. You cannot legislate peace. As surely as one side wins a ruling, the other side will work to get the ruling overturned.

The fight will go on and on and on.

Both sides have stated their case, loudly, redundantly, and ineffectively. Channel the energy you expend on fruitless debate into creating real change.

For example, one issue that was used against us, to deliberately divide and distract us, was women's rights. It's simple: Work together to respect and love all women. Pregnancy is a woman's right; it is personal, it is sacred, and many believe it is from God. Respect a woman's right to believe that babies are human beings from conception onward, even if you yourself don't agree. And on the flip side, if you support the pro-life moment, don't attempt to shame people into conversion, but instead extend your love to women in difficult situations.

Notice that I mentioned what *you* can do, not what your government can do. Remember, neonaticide and other atrocities weren't sanctioned by the government, but were criminal acts. Laws alone cannot protect women or babies. *You* need to step up! Clothe, feed, heal. Love women, work together. Divided you accomplish nothing but malice.

Now apply this same logic to *all* of the issues that divide us. Government can't resolve the issues that the American people have been fighting about for decades. Women's rights is only one example of hundreds of hot-button issues that we can't find resolution for. Our habit of expecting 'the system' to settle our disputes has created a backlog of unresolved issues that have divided our nation.

The more we expect government to fix our problems – to regulate or reverse regulation – the longer we ride the merry-go-round of division and malice. No, we don't need more government. We need more tolerance. *We need to stop hating our own people*.

I'll give you an example of what I mean. In pre-Big War America, after 911, persons of Islamic faith were feared to be terrorists simply because they were Muslim. I see a similar situation happening today with Christians– are all Christians bigoted, highly political and full of hate? Of course not! The actions of some have led to the fear and mistrust of all.

I'm telling you right now, and I hope you are all listening to me. If you don't get it that you must put your differences aside and love each other, you will be right back to where you started from. Can't you see that we are destroying ourselves? The fall of America isn't coming from outside, it's coming from within. We are doing this to our*selves*!

How can we avoid making the same mistakes we've made over the last three decades? For starters, don't mix religion and science with politics. The moment you ask government to regulate your values, you give up your freedom. You open the door for the horrors of misdirection that was RDAD. Solve your own problems!

Get off the Internet, get off the couch and *do* something about the things that you're riled up about. When you blast your views without respect for anyone else, you contribute to the hate that gave us a broken nation. Let's accept our differences instead of attempting—in vain—to convert others to our views. We can apply that energy into actually doing something to prevent tragedy from happening, into doing something to help those who have already fallen, and most of all to hold the hands of all who are currently struggling.

I know I'm beating a dead horse, but that horse has been rotting and stinking for a long time and yet we step right over it. Anger doesn't work. We must agree to disagree. We must respect each other even when we do not agree. I don't know how to say this more plainly, and I am flabbergasted that my final presidential address sounds like a 'welcome to kindergarten' lecture.

Incessant debate is a carping, a dripping, a persistent nagging. How patronizing of me that as your President I feel the most important thing to say to the American people is: Shut up.

And on that note, this is the last of my long-winded speeches: I am going to practice what I preach. I will shut up and do something!

One of the reasons why I am not running for re-election is because I can do great work as a private citizen. When I leave this office, I will step into my role as owner and CEO of a new independent investigation company, the likes of which you've never seen before. I am assembling a team of incredible people ready to tackle America's worst nightmares.

As President I've heard whispers of governmental experiments, advancements, and technological discovery that have made the hairs on my arms stand on end. Government has done a pathetic job of policing itself. Science is too big for us.

Remember what I said earlier? Science and religion shouldn't be regulated by government. These truths are *our* responsibility – we are all responsible for what we do to this planet, what we do to ourselves, and what we leave behind for future generations.

While I'm fighting the good fight against corruption and horrific futuristic technology, I ask that you too stand up and fight for something. Government grew big and became corrupt because we allowed it to happen – we didn't want to do our part. We wanted to live our lives in a bubble. It's not too late; it's never too late.

Volunteer at your local food bank. Donate your time to help children learn to read. Visit a nursing home. Post your progress on the Social Media Channel for all to see and be encouraged by. Think of the power we have if we all do our part. Together we can make a difference, I sincerely believe that. Don't fight with your words, as a coward, a thug or a fool. Fight with your good deeds; as a pacifist, as an activist, as a hero. Lay aside your bickering and get to work! There's a big world to save, beginning right here at home."

Ann paused to take a long draught of water. The rest of her speech made her "Play nicely together" opener seem like the spoonful of sugar to make the medicine go down. The truth, as Ann saw it, was that Americans were much more comfortable fighting about moral issues than facing up to economical ones. Ann knew that while the rest of her historic speech could impact generations to come, it could just as easily fall on deaf ears.

27

Ann prayed silently before launching into the meat of her speech. She coached herself with these thoughts: *This is the final stretch, you're almost done.* She looked directly into Camera One and spoke without looking at the teleprompter.

"But of course fixing what is broken in American government is not as simple as begging all of you to be kinder to one another. As we continue to reel from the complicated terrorist plot to financially take over our nation, we have to take a good look at ourselves. How did we get to such an insolvent state? How did we become so vulnerable? Well, I have a few thoughts that I'd like to share with you, and once again we find hate at the root of our problems.

In the days of Old America, in the dear idealistic past, Americans felt the romance of commercialism. Americans were great dreamers; anything could happen in America, and American ingenuity was rewarded financially. Living the good life was a worthy dream, even wholesome and honorable.

But somewhere along the way, we fell down. Greed and corruption changed us to the point that we began to equate wealth with evil, and wealthy Americans with people to fear, despise, and blame for all of our own shortcomings. Suddenly it was the rich who should pay for our nation's ills, and money itself was despicable in many aspects. Media portrayed the pursuit of wealth in the form of sharks, mobs, and corporate scum. Like a child whose parents believed the worst in him, our nation grew more and more corrupt – living up to our poor expectations. We have stopped seeing money as a blessing, and have focused on money as the root of all evil. As soon as we equated money with evil, money became evil.

I know I'm talking in metaphors and fuzzy grey emotional language, but I'm making my best attempt to inspire you to reach back into the past and draw from it the American spirit. You see, you have to decide how you want government to serve you while going forward, moving out of insolvency and into something new. Are you a capitalist nation? Are you a democracy? You can't hate money if you wish to rebuild this nation based on American dreams. You can't despise the wealthy or hate the poor. You must come together and desire the good in people.

Don't bite the hand that feeds, but instead encourage loyalty; loyalty to the nation and loyalty to you. How can you foster feelings of good will, cooperation and charity? Surely you are still an innovative people! Look to the old programs that have worked in the past. When did people pull together for the common good? When was it fashionable to be selfless and patriotic? I'm afraid that if you want to move forward, you must go backward, or risk losing forever what America once was.

We are battling a new kind of war, a financial one. You as a people have the power within you to raise the funds that can save your government and protect it from further attack. My best minds in finance have put together a number of packages that I hope you will be receptive to. However, much of that work will fall to the new administration. I can't even begin to address all of those issues today. I can only give you my best attempt to encourage you to fight for the American dream, and to work together during this crisis.

We were not always a nation of ugliness and division. We were once a people that other nations wanted to be: when the Americans came, others were happy to see us – we were kind, we were selfless, we were pure joy. Not without exception, of course, but we have been a nation that has birthed many heroes and heroines. May this be true of us again.

You're going to need American ingenuity to save yourselves. You're going to need to spend money—out of your own pocket, not government money. At this point you might be tuning me out, if I hadn't already lost you early on. This should get your attention: America is broke. Our government can't fix our problems.

Our government was bribed and sold to the highest bidder time and time again. Our food supply was tainted by greed; we poisoned our own people. Horrific acts of violence were committed; we disarmed our own people. When mass domestic violence continued unchecked, we pressed forward with increased gun control legislation, which as you know led to riots. Tensions escalated from protests about bill of rights violations, to what would become the worst massacre in American history—as over a dozen American cities rose up against armed government officials in our streets. Now let me say this again: The government can't fix our problems. Let's observe a moment of silence while you let that sink in."

Ann bowed her head and said nothing for sixty seconds of dead air that she counted inside her head. The videographers didn't know what to do. Camera One remained focused on the president for a full minute of complete inactivity. She then lifted her head and resumed her speech.

"Who can help us then? We can look beyond the government, to the church. Research by political scientists Putnam and Campbell attests that religiously observant Americans are more generous with their time and money. In this way, churches provide a necessary function in our nation outside of politics, transcending government for the good of all people.

Don't worry, I'm not advocating a national religion. I'm a firm believer of the separation of church and state, which I will repeat later on in my speech. However, is it the role of government to rally citizens to be charitable? I have tried to rally you, yet I fear that my words have fallen on deaf ears. The church is uniquely suited for this role, this necessary role, in a healthy society.

The church should open its arms to citizens in any sort of need, with complete disregard to politics. When the focus of the church is on healing its people, supporting its people, and fortifying its people to take care of each other, many shortcomings of politics and government can be overcome through acts of love rather than through force, malice, hatred and division. Dark days are coming—prepare now! When the soup lines are long, the church will be pressed upon to open its doors to feed the hungry.

We were once a religious nation, a solace for the persecuted. We can be again. Yet we continue to suffer from the great division between the extreme right and the extreme left, leaving citizens in the middle out in the cold; and of course all of our people suffer when the nation is in a perpetual state of disharmony.

Therefore I propose that we bring together the best minds; our scholars, our psychologists, our scientists, our religious leaders, our political analysts – you get the idea – bring them all together under one roof for a series of talks. I've already spoken to several dozen people from all walks of life, representing many faiths and ideologies, with the one common goal of reaching peaceful resolutions that will heal and unify our nation. If we are on board and fired up we can make changes, it is well within our power.

Before you all get your backs up let me be

clear: I'm not talking about converting anyone or watering down the religious beliefs of all Americans until what we are left with is a generic national religion that can be expressed on a bumper sticker! No, I am saying the polar opposite of those two extremes: I'm saying that we go back to respecting the *individual* religious freedoms of all Americans, that we honor the reason why our country was founded in the first place. Respect our differences, don't fight to make us all the same!

I am calling upon all of you to join us in these talks in your own communities, churches and homes. We can change the face of America, it is not too late. It is never too late. We were once a nation grateful for religious freedom. We can be that nation once again; we merely need to open our hearts to a new definition of what this means, and how we can work together to respect the faiths of all people. We can't do this alone— don't let your personal baggage cause you to reject sources of help!

Removing God from our nation is not the answer. Removing *self* is the answer. Becoming *selfless* is the answer, and it is the way to self-reliance: let's forget church and state for the moment. We have been so distracted by religion and government that we neglected the power we all have, as private citizens, to create change. When did it become fashionable to rely upon institutions to fix us?

While legislating fair wages, protecting vulnerable persons, and passing laws that protect us from all manner of criminal and heinous activity is a noble effort, and of course must be attempted, legislation is not nearly enough! Once our government has done all that it was established to do, continuing in that vein will strip the American people of the freedom we require to self-govern. We, the people, wear the ruby red slippers: we have had the power all along. We can work harder, do more, give more and love more.

I'm not saying that all of the talking we've done hasn't been beneficial; education and information are the first steps in creating change. But isn't it time for less talk and more action? Let's drop our extremism in favor of balance— don't be so quick to reject what you are afraid of.

When we are not grounded in our beliefs we are like boats adrift without an anchor; it's far too easy for us to go off course when the winds change or when larger boats toss us around in their wake. If we had been a stronger people perhaps we wouldn't have been so easily manipulated by the global campaign to distract us from the real problems we were facing, perhaps we would have seen the truth before so much destruction had already been done. I know we are hurting, but giving up is not the answer.

Our strength lies in our freedom, our faith, and in each other: draw upon those things now and fight! Preserve the separation of church and state: it is this separation that gives Americans religious freedom. And while keeping the two entities fully separate, utilize both! We will never agree with each other about what we should believe, but we must agree to protect our individual rights to believe it.

If you only take away one thing from my speech let it be this: Keep an open mind and contribute. I am asking this of you in my final request during what has been a remarkable term and a monumental chapter in American history.

However, I would be doing you a grave disservice if I left you with only these motivational sound bites. I'm afraid that I need your attention for a while longer."

President Ann Kinji opened the orange cloth-bound book titled "Democracy in America Volume 1" by Aexis de Tocqueville at the page she had bookmarked.

"'Democracy in America', published in 1961, has been quoted often these days. I'd like to highlight this section in particular. I know this is a tedious passage but please bear with me.

'... it is almost always by the abuse of its force, and the misemployment of its resources, that a democratic government fails. Anarchy is almost always produced by its tyranny or its mistakes, but not by its want of strength...

If ever the free institutions of America are destroyed, that event may be attributed to the unlimited authority of the majority, which may at some future time urge the minorities to desperation, and oblige them to have recourse to physical force. Anarchy will then be the result, but it will have been brought about by despotism.'"

Ann held her place in the book with her finger and spoke to Camera Two, causing a flurry of commotion for the videographers.

"Despotism isn't a word we use every day, so I'll define this term for you before continuing. Despotism is a form of government in which a single entity rules with absolute power; the implication is that despotism involves tyranny of some sort, in which the government, in this case the majority rule, suppresses the rights and freedoms of the citizens."

Ann opened the book and resumed reading from it. 'Mr. Hamilton expresses the same opinion in the Federalist, No. 51 when he states that it is of great importance in a republic not only to guard the society against the oppression of its rules, but to guard one part of society against the injustice of the other part. ... In a society, under the forms of which the stronger faction can readily unite and oppress the weaker, anarchy may as truly be said to reign as in a state of nature, where the weaker individual is not secured against the violence of the stronger.'"

The crinkly sound of pages being turned was picked up loudly by Ann's microphone. The tech team scrambled to balance the sound.

"I'll end with a Jefferson quote from later in this same section: 'The tyranny of the legislature is really the danger most to be feared, and will continue to be so for many years to come.'

I know this is dry, and that I've lost some of you. You may be wondering what this has to do with anything. My dear Americans, I'm afraid that what Aexis de Tocqueville wrote in 1961 is sadly something I need to warn you about.

We are ripe for a civil war. Yes, I know, first I told you that America is bankrupt, and now I am telling you that we are at the point of collapse. RDAD may have distracted us from the truth but it didn't change what the truth is. While some aspects of our national economy have improved, we are overall a sinking ship. The leaks created by corruption and bad management have put us in dire straits. As we point fingers and attempt to legislate solutions to our problems, we meanwhile continue to suffer.

We have been bitterly divided for so long that we have allowed our democracy to become oppressive, and the legislature has become a bully. If my desperate plea for you to come together as a nation, to love each other, to respect each other, and to resolve your differences goes unheeded, I must warn you that our country is just one spark away from setting off a powder keg of resentment that will result in a civil war. As each side blames the other for the woes of our nation, the economy being the most bitter pill for most people, we have set the stage for the minority to rise up against the majority rule. Popular and electoral vote will mean nothing as citizens wish to overthrow the tyranny of the majority rule.

I'm sorry to deliver such a dramatic and dire warning, but I must reiterate: if we stay on this course, we are headed for civil war in the not so distant future. Since there is no suitable transition from this bleak warning I'll simply say that I am finally drawing this speech to a close. Let me remind you that I gave you a clean slate in Congress. When I leave this office, the pre-Big War regime will be officially over—no more 'old boys' club. This is a second chance for America! What will you do with it? Will you trust government to take care of you, and when that fails will you attempt to use religion to legislate? Or will you give unto Caesar that which is Caesar's and worship freely separately from the government, rising up with courage to work hard as individuals; as innovators, healers, inventors, philanthropists, creators, teachers, leaders, parents, students—*citizens*?

Will you put decency ahead of profit? Will you be generous instead of holding back on what you have to offer? Will you push yourself harder when life deals you a difficult hand? Will you dare to dream—and will your dreams benefit others? I meant what I said: if you continue on your current path you will destroy each other. I love you, the American people, and I wish that no harm come to you. Thank you for allowing me the podium for such an extended period of time.

My dear Americans, it has been my greatest pleasure to serve you as your president. Beyond the presidency, you have taken me into your homes and into your hearts, as you have been in mine. I've thought long and hard about what I want to say to you in my last formal speech before the nation. In closing, I have decided to repeat, verbatim, the same closing paragraphs of the speech I delivered to you early on in my presidency:

Stop fighting each other. Let statues stand, let people pray, let flags fly. Agree that Love is more important than settling who is right. When I close with my final words, may you hear them not with contempt or division in your heart, but with the goodness I wish for you; to be well, stay safe, fill your heart with hope, and love one another.

And these, my final words: God Bless America."

28

"Agent Estep, I'd love to have you on my team. How does the private sector sound to you?" asked President Kinji.

"No disrespect to you, Madam President, but I want to stay on at the agency. In fact, I'm on my way now to receive my next field assignment, my first one in years sans Serena Waldo."

"Serena Wilcox," Ann corrected.

Serena explained, " He means Waldo, as in 'Where's Waldo?' because he spent so much time looking for me."

Estep reiterated, "Madam President, I do appreciate your offer, however the answer is a definite no."

Ann smiled sweetly. "Well, if you change your mind, I'll be here for a while longer."

When Estep was out of earshot Serena challenged Ann. "What did you do?"

Ann held up her hand. "He's just around the corner. He'll be back in three, two…"

Estep stormed past them. He then spun on his heels and walked back to where President Kinji was waiting for him. "He won't give me my assignment. They're giving me a desk job!"

Ann patted Estep lightly on the arm. "When you join my team you'll take lead in all field investigations."

Estep prepared to walk away.

Ann waved a carrot in front of his nose. "I'm sure I can arrange that you stay on with the agency, and work for us only on loan. Give it six months or so and I'm sure they'll let you back in the field."

"I'll still be on payroll here? It won't affect my standing with the agency?" Estep was listening.

Ann coaxed, "I'm sure of it. Consider it done."

Estep nodded, mumbled a thank you, shook her hand and left, but not without a parting withering look at Serena.

Serena watched Estep's back disappear out the door. She squinted her eyes at Ann. "*You* told them to give him desk duty, didn't you?"

Ann winked.

Serena laughed. "Well played. But when we are working together, promise me that you won't manipulate *me* like that."

"Oh I never make a promise I can't keep."

Serena decided to be honest about her feelings. "I do need to talk to you about something."

Ann nodded.

Serena took that as a green light. "I've been a stay at home mom for my kids' whole lives. These Covert Coffee and Bluebird adventures have been torture."

Ann looked genuinely puzzled. "All of your kids are older, right? Teenagers at least?"

"They're fine. It was temporary. But I won't

leave them like this again. If I'm going to partner with you I'll need to work from home."

"I see." Ann appeared to be studying the ceiling tiles. "Let's continue this at Laurey's."

Serena agreed. The two dark-haired petite women attracted attention from Cube employees as they walked the quarter mile of corridors and went up two flights of escalators to get to the food court. Laurey's sit-down restaurant sat in the outer ring, beyond the burger and taco stands.

Once seated at Laurey's they ordered drinks and an appetizer, and chatted about their personal lives for a while. Then Ann resumed their conversation. "First of all, you have misunderstood the situation. You won't be partnering with me, you'll be working for me. Consider me your President. Except instead of governing over the smallness of the United States I'll be dealing with the fate of the entire planet, and beyond."

Serena stared at Ann. She could see that she wasn't playing around. "What do you mean?"

"You'll find out."

"No, I don't think that I will. I've already

explained that I won't be accepting your offer unless I can work from home."

"You can do the research aspects from home. The field work will obviously need to be done in the field."

"I'm afraid I'm going to have to turn this opportunity down then." Serena took a bite of chicken from the appetizer platter. She figured she might as well enjoy this one last perk.

"Take time to think it over."

"I'm sorry, Ann, but I have sacrificed my career before and I'm definitely willing to do it again, no matter how great the opportunity you are offering me, I value my family life more."

"Even if it means passing up the opportunity to time travel?"

"What? Did you just say 'time travel'?"

Ann smiled.

"You're serious? What do you mean time travel?"

"You'll have to join my team if you want to find out. It's 'need to know'."

"I-I don't think I can pass this up. I don't know what to do. Time travel." Serena breathed deeply and counted to ten. Her mind was full of colors and sounds.

Ann folded her hands and made a steeple with her index fingers. "Your kids are well behaved, surely. And maybe they can be an asset? They could assist you?"

"Are you saying that I should bring my kids with me in the field; to be shot, abducted, or bludgeoned? I can't imagine Tom agreeing to this."

"Bring him along, he can protect the kids. And when have you been concerned about being bludgeoned?"

"You're saying my whole family should come with me into the field? You're messing with me now."

"No, I'm saying that I don't care what you do. The field work is not considered dangerous. You can bring the whole family if you want to. I'm only saying that you can't do the work from home."

"Time travel. I'd be a time traveler? How is that possible? Would I travel in a time machine like the T.A.R.D.I.S? What happens exactly?"

"Ah, well, 'need to know'. Trust me. Time travel is possible and it has been for at least a decade."

"What would be the purpose of me doing this? What exactly would I be investigating?"

"I can't tell you that. What I can say is that time travel technology has been abused from the start, from even before it began actually. I'm afraid you won't be on a pleasure trip. You'll be doing what you do best: solving crimes."

"Ah, the truth comes out. I don't see how I can bring my family into this. We're back to me saying that I can't accept your offer."

"The bad guys are long gone- they are locked up or dead. You'll only be figuring out what they did and why so that we can stop some of the damage from happening. You'll report what you find, that's all. No face-time with criminals. Consider it a genealogical project: Perfectly safe."

"I'll talk it over with Tom."

"Yes, do that."

Serena frowned, biting her lower lip. She hated making heavy decisions. If only there was an obvious factor that would tip the scales toward going one way or the other. She turned to leave.

"Oh Serena?"

Serena stopped.

"You might want to show this figure to Tom. This is my proposal." Ann handed her a slip of paper.

Serena gasped. "Wow, that's a lot of zeros. I have to admit that it would be good to have an annual salary. This is more than I've ever made from contract work."

"Who said anything about annual? That's your *monthly* take-home."

Serena blurted, "I'm in." Then she nearly ran out of the restaurant. Once outside the doors she sang, "I'm traveling, I'm traveling!"

BLUEBIRD FLOWN

EPILOGUE

Serena Wilcox takes on a new adventure as a time travel investigator in Project Scarecrow while working for former United States President Ann Kinji; President, Founder, and CEO of GSI (Gödel Solution Institute).

Scientists have discovered that inside every human brain are memory impressions of the past, present and future; a complete record of one's life from birth to death. While most of us can only access the present and part of the past, people with brain anomalies can access all past memory impressions and/or have what was previously thought of as psychic ability. Through blood and spinal fluid samples from centenarians and newborns, scientist gained access to memory impressions of 100+ years into the past, and potentially as many years into the future.

Digitized memory impressions, combined with quantum physics and teleportation, made possible time travel. Naturally, in Serena's world, time travel technology was immediately abused. In Project Scarecrow, criminal investigation takes Serena to the past, present and future.

The Serena Wilcox Mysteries Time Travel Trilogy will take you backwards and forwards with favorite returning characters and suspense that will keep you turning pages to the end.

Look for Serena Wilcox Mystery #7,
Book #1 in the Time Travel Trilogy

Project Scarecrow

Fall of 2013

The Serena Wilcox Mysteries
By Natalie Buske Thomas

Stay in the loop!

www.nataliebuskethomas.com

Author Notes

As the Serena Wilcox Dystopian Trilogy comes to an end I realize that I've been holding my breath. *Angels Mark* took me about three years to write. I was dabbling and unfocused, partly because my three children were young at the time, but also because I was nervous about re-entering the writing scene after ten years of absence.

About a quarter of the way through *Angels Mark* I experienced multiple losses that led to spiritual and personal growth (the death of my mother being one of those). During that time, *Angels Mark* seemed to write itself. Writing a heavy-hitting political thriller with controversial themes was never my intention. I simply wanted to write a good mystery that showed improvement from my previous work.

My mystery became more of a thriller and eventually the word "dystopian" was added to it as well. The Angels Mark project had evolved into something quite different from what it was in the beginning.

Within a few months after my return to writing and publishing, *Angels Mark* hit Amazon's bestselling list. The ride on the bestselling list was brief, but over thirty thousand people downloaded my book and I enjoyed the best paycheck I'd ever received for my artistic endeavors. I had arrived!

Unfortunately people cut me down almost faster than I rose. I knew that some readers would find fault, but the venom in which they found fault took me aback—few attacks had anything to do with my writing or the story; most were personal, irrelevant or religious/political (or all three of these). I even feared for my family's safety if I were to continue writing these books.

My daughter said that I must be doing it right if both the extreme left and the extreme right are unhappy with me. There was nothing fun about being hated: I wanted to get off this ride.

That was my state of being while I was writing *Bluebird Flown*. My attitude comes across in ways both subtle and obvious, mainly through the character of Serena Wilcox. I identified with Serena the most when nearing the end of *Bluebird Flown*.

Like Serena, I just wanted to "go home". I wanted to return to the life I had before *Angels Mark* was released. I wanted this experience to end. But then again, like Serena, I can't resist the allure of a time travel adventure. Some of my favorite books when I was a kid were: *Danny Dunn, Time Traveler*; *Charlie and the Great Glass Elevator*; *A Wrinkle in Time*, all of the Frank Baum *Oz* books; and of course *The Chronicles of Narnia*. I'm thrilled to have time-traveling sci-fi adventures as a grownup too: my son is a devoted Doctor Who fan; he insisted that the whole family watch it with him and now I'm hooked!

The time-travel sci-fi genre is also where my early writing experiences came from. My first published story was an alternate time, space and dimension sci-fi adventure called *The Personalities**. I won my high school writing contest for that story, ten dollars! It was the first time I made money as an author. Later on down the road, when I was in my twenties, I wrote the second book of the Serena Wilcox Mysteries, *Virtual Memories*, featuring sci-fi alternate reality. It's been a long time since I've thrown myself into that genre. Oh how I look forward to escaping into the Serena Wilcox Time Travel Trilogy!

I'm prepared to put myself into this with both

feet with research and back-story like I did with the dystopian trilogy. My reward for this effort will be the fun I'll have writing as Serena, Estep, Beav, Lehman, Ann Kinji and the new characters Jo and Joe. And of course I'll enjoy inventing revolting villains and outrageous situations, plot twists, cliffhangers (moohoohaha!) and everything else that makes the Serena Wilcox series what it is. The series is bigger than me now, it's taken on a life of its own and it now belongs to all of us.

There's a sparkling future waiting for me, should I choose to accept the challenge of writing the Serena Wilcox Time Travel Trilogy. Yes, there may be danger—if there's no risk involved, are we truly living? I'm in. And there's a new adventure waiting for you too. Are you in? Sing with me: *We're traveling, we're traveling!*

The Personalities story is available to read (free) online: www.NatalieBuskeThomas.com

ABOUT THE AUTHOR

Natalie Buske Thomas is an author, artist and entertainer. She is working on her first music single and is currently traveling with her new Serena Wilcox Time Travel Trilogy.

PROJECT SCARECROW:

Serena investigates horrific crimes of science and technology; traveling through time and space to repair the damage and save the world before it's too late. Meanwhile Speaker of the House Joseph Smythe becomes the next American president, but does he get the girl? Ann Kinji, Estep, Lehman, and the Beav welcome Jo from Ireland to the team. New adventures await – are you in?

Twitter: @writernbt
Pinterest: @writernbt
Facebook: Natalie Buske Thomas
Easy "follow" buttons are on the authors' website; as well as free games, news about Natalie's books, oil paintings, comics and more:

NATALIE BUSKE THOMAS

www.nataliebuskethomas.com